SPECIAL MESSAGE TO READERS

This book is published under the auspices of

THE ULVERSCROFT FOUNDATION

(registered charity No. 264873 UK)

Established in 1972 to provide funds for research, diagnosis and treatment of eye diseases. Examples of contributions made are: —

A Children's Assessment Unit at Moorfield's Hospital, London.

•

Twin operating theatres at the Western Ophthalmic Hospital, London.

•

A Chair of Ophthalmology at the Royal Australian College of Ophthalmologists.

•

The Ulverscroft Children's Eye Unit at the Great Ormond Street Hospital For Sick Children, London.

You can help further the work of the Foundation by making a donation or leaving a legacy. Every contribution, no matter how small, is received with gratitude. Please write for details to:

THE ULVERSCROFT FOUNDATION,
The Green, Bradgate Road, Anstey,
Leicester LE7 7FU, England.
Telephone: (0116) 236 4325

In Australia write to:
THE ULVERSCROFT FOUNDATION,
c/o The Royal Australian and New Zealand
College of Ophthalmologists,
94-98 Chalmers Street, Surry Hills,
N.S.W. 2010, Australia

Roger Silverwood lives on the outskirts of Barnsley. After National Service he entered the toy trade where he became a sales director. Aged 50 he went into business with his wife as an antique dealer specializing in Victorian jewellery until he retired in 1997.

THE UMBRELLA MAN

When an arsonist and murderer threatens to set fire to the local MP's home, Detective Inspector Michael Angel has two suspects: one has disappeared, the other is locked up in a cell. But what do twelve umbrellas found hanging from his bedroom ceiling mean? Will the umbrella man be able to execute his threat while still in police custody? Meanwhile, the murder of a famous stage magician's assistant appears to be a copy of an unsolved crime committed twenty-five years previously. Could both cases be related? The DI must race against the clock to unravel this strange and chilling mystery.

Books by Roger Silverwood
Published by The House of Ulverscroft:

DEADLY DAFFODILS
IN THE MIDST OF LIFE
THE MAN IN THE PINK SUIT
MANTRAP

ROGER SILVERWOOD

THE UMBRELLA MAN

Complete and Unabridged

ULVERSCROFT
Leicester

First published in Great Britain in 2007 by
Robert Hale Limited
London

First Large Print Edition
published 2007
by arrangement with
Robert Hale Limited
London

British Library CIP Data

Silverwood, Roger
    The umbrella man.—Large print ed.—
    Ulverscroft large print series: mystery
    1. Angel, Michael (Fictitious character)—Fiction
    2. Police—England—Yorkshire—Fiction
    3. Detective and mystery stories 4. Large type books
    I. Title
    823.9'14 [F]

    ISBN 978–1–84617–977–8

Published by
F. A. Thorpe (Publishing)
Anstey, Leicestershire

Set by Words & Graphics Ltd.
Anstey, Leicestershire
Printed and bound in Great Britain by
T. J. International Ltd., Padstow, Cornwall

This book is printed on acid-free paper

DOWDESWELL'S BOOK OF MAGICK SPELLS

or Grimoire A.D. 1646

Also INVOCATIONS, CHARMS, RUNIC SYMBOLS, ARBATEL, PURIFICATION, TRANSCENDENTAL MAGICK AND ALSO INCLUDING THE SEVEN MYSTERIOUS ORISONS.

Spell XII: To put a man under a woman's spell.

Steal ten hairs from the crown of a fair haired
    damsel, more beautiful, more powerful be
    the spell,
Heat them in an iron pot, with water from the
    well.
Add the urine of two virgins, the skins of four
    frogs mix,
A lock of the hair of the man hisself, and the
    wings of honey bees, six.
Remove one stocking to cover your eyes and
    speak the incantation.
This spell will bind the greatest man
    regardless of his station.
Let the potion cool and bring it where he lie
    the night abed.
The great words of Awolla in the darkness
    should be said.

Keep this on the tricksit, for two days, incanting thus:

Awolla, Awolla, Awolla, testi, canut, muss.

Take in your hands a bunch of heavy pollen clover,

Weave fresh grass in your hair and speak the spell again thrice over.

Smear the potion round the house, where sleeps the indifferent male.

This spell doth bind forever and is not known to fail.

Set twixt midnight and the third hour on a Friday, in the month of May,

Will deliver him to your chamber in a full moon and a day.

1

Theatre Royal, Blackchester, North Yorkshire.
23 February 1981

'And now, ladies and genamen,' said a voice over the theatre loudspeaker, 'for your delectation, Mysto and his beautiful assistant, Imelda, will re-enact the famous scene from *The Arabian Nights*, known as 'Caliph and the Slave Girl'. I thenk you.'

There was a thud through the loudspeaker as the stage-manager put the microphone clumsily onto his cap on the desk-top on the prompt side of the wings and rushed off to close a door behind him that was sending a cold draught straight onto his half-eaten fish and chips, which were in their paper on the electrician's stool in front of the switchboard.

The theatre orchestra began to play *The Sheik From Araby*, the audience settled down and gazed at the stage wide-eyed with anticipation, the front-of-house lights dimmed and the proscenium curtain went up.

The set was smart but very basic. At the back of the stage was a closed burgundy

1

curtain. In front of that, positioned in the middle of the prompt side, was a narrow cardboard pillar painted to represent marble, and on the other side, a reproduction oriental couch.

In the centre at the front of the stage was a big man standing with his feet slightly apart and his thick, bare arms folded. He was wearing a huge turban, yellow silk waistcoat, white shirt, cummerbund and red baggy trousers. That was Mysto the magician: the leading magic man in the UK at that time, hardly ever off the television screen and when he was, he was working whatever entertainment organizations were still booking live acts, in theatres, seaside piers, town halls, summer seasons, nightclubs and wherever he could economically work his illusions and sell enough tickets to make a satisfactory profit.

On the couch, looking as delicious as an over-sugared advertisement for Turkish delight, was the smiling, beautiful slave girl, played by Imelda. She was dressed in a gilt tiara, tiny gilt bra, pink baggy trousers and high-heeled gilt sandals, making Zsa Zsa Gabor look like a bag-lady. Imelda smiled, stretched and squirmed at the audience to show off her perfect figure in such a way as to stir even the coldest male.

Mysto bowed graciously to the audience, then went off the stage via the wings and returned immediately, carrying two ordinary-looking plain wooden trestles. He placed them at the centre of the stage, four feet apart. Then he brought on a wooden box the shape and size of a coffin. He carried it easily; it didn't weigh much. It was greatly decorated, with round and oval coloured plastic shapes that glittered and reflected the stage lights. He rotated it ostensibly casually, but it was really to suggest to the audience that it was a simple wooden box. He placed it across the trestles on its side with the hinged lid open to show the audience it was empty. Then he turned the box on to its back and left the lid open.

When Imelda saw the box arrive, she pretended to look afraid of it. She acted herself dizzy to show the audience that there was something frightening about the box and that she was afraid of it.

Mysto went over to her, grasped her roughly by the hand. She screamed and resisted. He brought her to the front of the stage and from out of his cummerbund pulled a white scarf. When she saw it, she screamed again and protested all the more. He placed it over her eyes and was fastening it when she broke away from him. She ran around the stage being chased by him. Eventually, she pretended to hide behind the 'marble' pillar, but he found her, put the blindfold over her eyes and mouth, fastened it, pulled her roughly out from behind the pillar, then picked her up bodily, when she obligingly kicked her legs, screamed and threw out her arms in useless protest as he lowered her into the box. She screamed some more, kicked out her arms and legs as he struggled to close the hinged lid. When she was in the box and the lid down, he produced a chain, wrapped it round the box tightly several times, fastened it with a giant padlock, then produced a pink silk sheet and draped it neatly over the box. He fussed over the position of the sheet, making changes to its exact position until he was satisfied that it was where he wanted it to be and was perfectly symmetrical, then he turned to face the audience.

Immediately, the orchestra stopped playing *The Sheik From Araby*, the drummer gave a mighty drum-roll followed by a clash of cymbals, and then at the side of the theatre, in a box above the orchestra stalls in the glare of two spotlights standing on a raised platform appeared the beautiful, striking figure of Imelda, laughing and waving the white scarf at the big man on the stage. He played up to her, looked amazed and stared at the coffin-shaped box on the stage in disbelief. He dashed over to it, hastily whipped off the pink sheet, unlocked the padlock, unravelled the chain, opened the lid, looked more astonished, turned the box over to face the audience, to show, of course, that it was empty.

The audience enjoyed the magic and applauded appreciatively.

Mysto smiled his thanks, took a slow bow, blew a toothy kiss at Imelda, who waved back graciously and acknowledged the applause as the proscenium curtain came down.

The spotlights on Imelda were cut. She stepped off the platform and rapidly disappeared through the box door into the theatre corridor.

The orchestra struck up a Souza march. The front-of-house lights went up and the delighted, happy audience began making its way to the aisles and exits.

Meanwhile, behind the curtain, Mysto had pulled off and was carrying a fulsome black wig inside the turban. Scratching his itching scalp as he moved the coffin-shaped box and the trestles off the stage to a position near the stage door for collection the next day, he stomped wearily off the stage and turned down the corridor behind the backcloth to his dressing-room, which was the third and last room at the end.

As he reached the door, the stage-manager saw him and smiled.

'Great audience tonight, Mr Butcher?'

'Yes, indeed,' the magician said, giving him a toothy smile.

'You knocked them dead.'

'Yes,' he said.

Blackchester, North Yorkshire.
24 February 1981

It was after 2 a.m. and the sky was as black as an undertaker's cat when a Mercedes without lights purred slowly up the alley at the side of the Theatre Royal, Blackchester and came quietly to a stop. Its tailgate was precisely in line with the sign that read STAGE DOOR. The driver, a big man in a black overcoat and black Homburg hat, pulled on the handbrake and switched off the ignition. He stayed motionless in the car for a full five minutes, occupying his time glancing up and down the street and listening, while licking his lips. His eyes flitted from side to side, like those of a lost hare waking up in a kitchen full of jugs.

When the street fell still, he silently slid out of the car, glided up the three steps to the stage door, unlocked it and slipped smoothly into the theatre.

Two minutes later, in the best traditions of the profession, he appeared silently, like magic, on the top step at the stage door carrying a lifeless bundle wrapped in something black. He glanced down the alley and listened. He could hear only a car revving in the distance and briefly see and hear two drunks leaning on each other, passing the front of the theatre, murdering *Danny Boy*. He waited until they were out of view, then he transferred the bundle to the boot of the car, quickly covering a shapely cold foot that fell out of the black cover as he gently lowered it. He closed the boot, returned to the stage door, locked it and then slipped into the driver's seat of the car.

The diesel started first time with the slightest clunk and the Mercedes glided out into the street. The side-lights came on. The car was soon out of the town and arrived at a T junction and a signpost that offered the choice of Harrogate or Leeds and Bradford. The driver chose Harrogate and once on the straight, he put the smooth diesel engine through its paces. He had no idea where he was heading. He had to dispose of a young woman's body. And he didn't want it being traced back to him. He had thought that the wooded countryside offered the best dumping ground. After driving for about twenty minutes he checked the clock on the dash: it showed 3.32. That seemed far enough. There was no traffic about. He slowed and looked for a quiet B road. He found one on his left and turned down it. A mile along there and he came unexpectedly to a stone bridge. He stopped the car, got out and looked down over the old stone bridge wall. Beneath him, in the dim light he could make out three sets of railway lines. One of the lines was a siding on which there was a long train of wagons. He moved further along the bridge and could see that the wagons were loaded with something like lime, sand or aggregate, also, and more to the point, he could position himself directly over the top of one of the wagons. He rubbed his chin.

High Street, Bromersley, South Yorkshire, UK. Monday, 3 April 2003.

The church clock struck one. It was pitch-black and as still as the juice at a Methodist wedding when Taffy Didmot smeared the rear window of The Old Curiosity Shop with Tate and Lyle's sweetest and most golden, licked his gloved fingers clean of the sticky stuff and wiped them on a piece of shirtlap, rashly thrown away by his wife and prudently rescued by him from the bin. He unfolded the sheet of brown paper that had that very morning arrived at his house wrapped round his missis's order from Grattan's, and slapped it across the window pane. He took a screwdriver out of his inside pocket and gently tapped out the glass, making little less noise than undertaker Elias Edmondson's chisel made when cutting corner joints in a coffin.

Taffy Didmot was through the window and inside the shop in a second. He switched on his pencil torch and made his way across the room. He found the shop door and directed the light upward. There he spotted a metal rod projecting from the top of the door. Six inches away from the rod, suspended from the ceiling, was a bell on a spring, strategically sited so that it would receive a hearty clout by the rod each time the door was opened.

He pushed the stuffed grizzly bear in rampant pose away from the front of an old upright piano with brass candlestick-fittings screwed each side of the fitted music stand, to find underneath the keyboard a substantial stool. He dragged it into position. He stood on the seat and reached up to the bell-hammer and bent it downwards out of the path of the bell. He dragged the stool back and flashed the torch at the door. There were two heavy bolts, one at the top of the door and another at the bottom; he withdrew them, making the noise of a hungry mouse in an undertaker's pantry. It caused him some concern. He froze and listened for a full minute before continuing operations. Below the doorknob was an old, sturdy, five-lever lock. He pulled out the screw-driver, applied it to the big screws on the doorjamb, removed the lock and in two minutes the door was open and Harry Hull, his brother-in-law, who had been hovering outside, sneaked in.

'Quietly, Harry.'

'Good stuff here, Taff,' he whispered, waving his torch at the reflecting silverware, pottery and glass pieces in the display cabinets that lined most of the wall space in the overstocked, cluttered little shop.

'Shhhh. And keep that torch down,' Taffy replied and began tapping lightly on the walls with the screwdriver handle. He tapped between oil-paintings, stuffed animal heads, a displayed Union Jack, a copper hunting-horn and a tigerskin. In a little while he found the echoing sound he had been searching for. He tore down the Union Jack disdainfully and flashed his pencil light to reveal the front of a

10

small, black safe built into the wall.

'Ah,' Taffy Didmot whispered excitedly. 'It's here, Harry.'

He peered at the dial, the brass handle and the small black circular door.

Harry Hull came across and joined him. The two men stared closely at the safe for a few seconds.

'Can you open it? That's the thing.'

'Dunno, man. Dunno, do I?'

'It'll be a six-figure combination.'

'I can see *that*,' Taffy said irritably. He reached into his inside pocket and pulled out a stethoscope.

Harry Hull felt his pockets and took out a pencil and a pad.

It was going to be a long night.

★ ★ ★

It was two and a quarter hours later, at 3.15 a.m. when Taffy Didmot sighed, tapped the tips of his fingers together excitedly, turned the brass handle and confidently pulled the door of the safe. It opened obediently.

Harry Hull's eyes shone.

'I knew you could do it, Taffy,' he said excitedly.

Paper money was sticking out. The little wall safe was crammed full with the stuff, some in wrappers and some just shoved in roughly.

Didmot took out a Tesco's plastic carrier-bag he had brought specially for the purpose, unfolded it and held it open while Hull eagerly pulled out the cash and packed it inside.

At length Didmot said, 'Is that it?'

'There's a bag at the back and something hard on the bottom. A book, I think.'

He pulled out a linen bag. It was only small, but heavy for its size and it rattled. He opened the mouth of the bag and shone the torch on to it. It reflected yellow.

'Sovereigns! Gold sovereigns!'

'Shhh!'

Didmot snatched the bag off him and dropped it into the carrier.

Then Hull reached inside for the book and manoeuvred it out of the mouth of the safe.

'What's that?'

'It's an old book, I think.'

'A book?' he said mockingly. 'We don't want that. Come on. Let's go.'

Didmot stood up, shook down the contents of the Tesco carrier and flashed his torch around to see if he had left anything.

Meanwhile, Hull rested the old leather-bound book on the top of the piano and flashed his torch on the cover. He could just make out the words that had once glowed richly in gold leaf: *Dowdeswell's Book of Spells*.

His eyes shone like a child's on a Christmas morning.

He stuffed the book under his coat.

London UK. Saturday, 2 p.m. 21 June 2003

The sun shone brightly on 2000 people, as they shouted slogans, waved crudely made banners, sometimes dangerously, while tramping through the iron gates of Hyde Park on their journey to Trafalgar Square.

It was an unruly crowd, some brandishing cans of lager or other alcoholic drink with which they regaled themselves on the journey. Many displayed large areas of skin with blue-and-red tattoos of gory scenes of wars and dragons and other subjects of which their grandmothers would not have approved. Some young women wore clothes showing more flesh than their mothers would have revealed at the side of a swimming pool. Safety-pins and other metal appendages decorated faces, ears, navels and other places.

The banners displayed a mix of politics and social discontent. Vote for the Freedom party.

Down with dictators. Liberty for the people. No to nanny state. Ban the drug laws. Let the people decide. Father at 14. Fight at 14. Vote at 14. Heroes take heroin. Cocaine for conquerors. We're fit for amphetamines. Lee Wong — freedom fighter. Your next member of parliament. Wong is right for Westminster. Lee Wong will defend the little people. Get out of Europe. Cut ties with US. Shut Guantanamo Bay. Stand on our own feet. Abolish the Lords. Tax the rich — help the poor. Wong rights wrongs. Et cetera.

At the head of the procession a handsome young man with oriental features and jet-black hair, in a dark suit and a spotless open-necked white shirt, was being pushed on a platform the size of a small stage with rubber-tyred wheels. He was smiling and waving his arms in the air enthusiastically. A banner erected above his head read: 'You can't go wrong — vote for Lee Wong!'

Down the street, coming towards them, was another procession of forty police on horseback in bright-yellow coats and armoured helmets. The leader went through the crowd and up to the platform on which Lee Wong was being transported. Wong's pushers stopped pushing and glared up at the mounted policeman.

A few phrases were exchanged, then Wong

turned to the crowd, waved a hand in the air, made a short speech and yelled something only they could understand.

Then all hell was let loose.

The marchers began to attack the policemen on horseback, who in response drew their asps and defended themselves. They were eventually forced to withdraw but reinforcements in defensive Range Rovers arrived and after two hours of fighting and general commotion order was reached.

There were a few casualties on both sides and Lee Wong was arrested. There were five outstanding charges against him and a further four charges were brought against him that day. They were: disturbing the peace, holding a public meeting in the city of London without a licence, assaulting a police officer and inciting an affray.

A month later, he was tried, found guilty and sent to Armley Prison in Leeds for five years. He served two years and nine months and was released on 10 March 2006.

Bromersley, South Yorkshire, UK. 2 p.m. Saturday 8 April 2006

'Now we come to lot seventy-two,' said the red-faced auctioneer from the rostrum. 'A doll.'

15

Some of the crowd murmured their lack of interest.

'Much sought after,' he added as an afterthought.

The bored warehouseman in a brown overall held up an ugly, shapeless nondescript lump of wood and rags with a brightly painted face more frightening than Dr Crippen in the altogether.

'Very old . . . could be antique?'

There were chuckles and jeers from the crowd.

'Who'll start me off at five pounds?'

Mocking smiles and thrifty silence was the crowd's response.

'Two pounds then,' Mr Snatchpole, the auctioneer suggested.

There were more jeers and laughter.

'If I don't get a bid, I shall pass it,' he said challengingly.

A small voice at the front said something. Snatchpole heard it.

'A pound?'

He sniffed, then said, 'Very well.'

A woman's voice at the back suddenly called out, 'Five pounds.'

'Five pounds, Mrs Wilde, thank you,' the auctioneer said with a smile.

On hearing her name, everybody turned round.

Imelda Wilde was a tall, long-legged pretty woman in her forties, much admired and very well-known in Bromersley; she brought scowls from women and smiles from men. She had the face of Helen of Troy and a backside that stopped traffic.

The women murmured their opinions; the men sat quiet. Some even smiled.

The small voice at the front instantly whispered, 'Ten pounds.'

'Ten pounds, miss,' Snatchpole bellowed. 'Thank you.'

'Twenty-five pounds!' Imelda Wilde called.

'Fifty pounds,' said the small voice at the front.

'Did you say fifty pounds, miss?' said the auctioneer, beaming.

'Yes, sir.'

'What's your name, miss?'

'Maureen Goldstein.'

'Thank you, miss. Fifty pounds . . . here on the front row,' he said looking back at Imelda Wilde.

The crowd were silent and awestruck. Some stood up from their seats to peer at the diminutive bidder on the front row.

'A hundred pounds,' Imelda Wilde called out.

A man's voice suddenly called out from the back, 'A hundred and fifty.'

Snatchpole's eyebrows shot up.

'A discerning gentleman, I see. Fresh bidder. It's Mr Jamieson. Thank you, sir.'

The crowd turned to look round at a handsome man standing at the rear of the hall.

He was very well-dressed, looked superior and knew it. He grinned back at the crowd. He was the owner of an establishment in Bromersley called 'The Old Curiosity Shop.' It was reputed to sell everything unusual, works of art, curios; you name it, he sold it. The shop used also to be a pawnbroker's until the law made the pickings less rich, and gave the poor a more sporting chance of recovering their possessions at a reasonable rate.

'I've got a hundred and fifty pounds,' Snatchpole said, sticking back his shoulders and scanning the faces of the crowd for more bids.

'Two hundred pounds,' whispered Maureen Goldstein.

Snatchpole blinked and said: 'Two hundred pounds, I have on the front row. Thank you, miss.'

Snatchpole looked at Jamieson who shook his head and turned away. He then looked in the direction of Imelda Wilde, whose bright eyes twinkled as she touched her chin thoughtfully.

He caught her eye.

'Two hundred and ten?' he asked.

She flashed a finger with a red-painted nail at the end of it and nodded.

He looked down at Maureen Goldstein.

'Two hundred and twenty, miss?'

She shook her head and looked down at the floor.

Snatchpole looked around the room, then across at Imelda Wilde, banged down the gavel and said, 'Two hundred and ten pounds, thank you.'

There were mutters of disapproval from some of the women, smiles from the men . . . then the crowd fell silent.

Imelda Wilde left her seat, smiling, and made for the office.

Detective Inspector Michael Angel and his wife, who were sitting on the back row, had witnessed the sale of the strange-looking doll. Angel turned to his wife, Mary, and said, 'What do you think to that, lass? Two hundred and ten pounds for that ugly-looking thing. And it would frighten any child to death!'

'It's *not* a toy,' Mary said, wrinkling her nose. 'Anyway, what would any decent person want with a thing like that?' she added with a sniff. 'Not a toy for a child to play with anyway.'

'Is it . . . to stick pins in?'

'No. That's voodoo. It's a sort of . . . talisman for a certain sort of people.'

'What sort of people?'

'I don't know exactly. Astrology and stuff. People who believe in that sort of thing. Like a good-luck charm.'

'It's so ugly. I should think it's a *bad*-luck charm.'

'Listen, Michael. Our lot's coming up next.'

2

On the following Monday morning Detective Inspector Michael Angel drove his BMW into the yard behind Bromersley police station and parked it next to a white Ford van with *Gaimster & Gibson, ventilation engineers* painted on the side. He fed his card into the rear-door lock of the station, it clicked open and he let himself into the building. He made his way up the corridor and arrived promptly in his office at 8.28 a.m. He had hardly riffled through the post on his desk when there was a knock at the door.

He bawled, 'Come in,' and looked up from the pile.

It was Ahmed Ahaz, a handsome young Indian with a ready smile. He looked very smart in his new PC uniform.

'Good morning, sir.'

'You're back, lad,' Angel said with a grin. 'We've missed you.'

Ahmed smiled.

'Everything has been going smoothly. We are just getting used to it. You know, lad, I think, at a pinch, the force could just about manage without you,' he said drily.

Ahmed understood that Angel was teasing him. He knew he was genuinely pleased to see him again. There was nothing artificial or capricious about him. Ahmed Ahaz knew that DI Angel was as predictable as traffic lights.

'Sit down, lad. You're making the place look untidy.'

'Thank you, sir. I've seen the ACC and he says I've to report back to you.'

Ahmed had served under Angel for two years as a police cadet and had, following his eighteenth birthday, been to police college in Durham for twelve weeks. He had now graduated to the dizzy heights of probationer police constable.

'Ahmed,' he said with a smile. 'How did you get on at Aykley Heads then, lad?'

'All right, sir.'

'And how did you do in the exams?'

'Not bad, sir,' Ahmed said, trying to look modest.

The competition was intense. There were over sixty would-be policemen in every intake.

'Well?' Angel said impatiently.

Ahmed rubbed his mouth awkwardly.

'I was third, sir,' he said trying to conceal a smile.

Angel was impressed but he didn't show it.

'Mmmm,' he said rubbing his chin. 'I was

top, in my day. That was at Hendon. Not bad, I suppose. Well, no point in hanging about, lad. You'd better start off by making me a proper cup of tea.'

★ ★ ★

Angel knocked on the door.

'Come in,' the superintendent yelled.

'You wanted me, sir?' Angel looked across at the tall, skinny man with the bushy red, black and white eyebrows on the balding turnip-shaped head. Superintendent Harker was a miserable man. He looked as if he had swallowed a bag of nails, and, indeed, it seemed he had one stuck between his teeth and was trying with a fingernail to release it.

'Ah. Yes. Come in. Sit down. Did you know that those huge wagons of the Eastern Power and Gas Company, fully kitted out with a compressor and ladders and all the gubbins cost over a hundred thousand pounds each?' Superintendent Harker said.

'No, sir,' Angel replied, wrinkling his nose. He tried to look interested. He wasn't much concerned with how much they cost. He couldn't see the point. He hadn't a use for one so he had no immediate thoughts of making a purchase.

'That's fully equipped with power tools for

digging trenches, replacing gas pipes and pretty well most emergency work that might be needed on call.'

Angel nodded futilely, trying to work out the point of the question.

Harker said: 'Well, one has gone missing. It's been missing about three weeks. You knew about it, of course? It's been on standing orders.'

'Oh yes,' Angel lied. He hardly ever read standing orders. There was so much to read and memorize in his job. Reports and requests for info flooded in from the Home Office, other UK forces, foreign police forces, as well as domestically generated bumf.

'It has actually been seen, in broad daylight, driven around Bromersley.'

'Oh. Really, sir?' Angel said, trying to sound interested.

'Sir Tristram Shepherd is on the board of the Eastern Power and Gas Company, and he was telling the chief all about it last night at their annual ball.'

Angel nodded knowingly. That explained it all. That was why Superintendent Harker had suddenly taken an interest in the vehicle and its whereabouts. The chief constable had no doubt buttonholed him 'twixt martinis, asking him to try to exercise his influence over the robbery. He had told the superintendent, and the super was passing it down to the lackey.

'Taken from their secured yard behind the wholesale market . . . during the night. Beats me what anyone wants with it. It's not the sort of thing young lads would be interested in . . .'

'I'll watch out for it, sir. Shouldn't be hard to spot.'

Harker eyed him suspiciously: Angel wasn't usually so compliant. The superintendent might have felt that he was getting through to him after eight years. He was still contemplating a reply when the phone rang. He reached out for it.

'Harker. Yes?'

The conversation was brief and serious. The superintendent's small, black eyes glowered like those of an eagle.

'Right, sir,' he said at the conclusion of the call.

'That was the ACC,' he said sombrely, replacing the handset. 'Another fire at an MP's home. That's the second. This time it's Fred Charlesworth, MP for Breston North. Getting nearer all the time. House almost burned out. Six appliances. The *au pair* badly injured . . . taken by air ambulance to hospital . . . severely burned. The main road between Breston and Bromersley is blocked. That's the second member of parliament to have his home attacked by an arsonist.'

Angel blinked. It certainly was a serious matter. Nobody should live in fear of being burned out of their own home. Organized arson of this magnitude wasn't that common a crime. Targeting MPs, it was bound to be politically motivated.

Harker said: 'Of course, it's that young hothead, Lee Wong again. He's only been out of Armley a month or more. Let's get him put away permanently. Last known address . . . the Golden Cockerel. The ACC wants *us* to bring him in. There's nobody else. Uniformed are all at this cup-tie.'

'Right, sir.'

★　★　★

Angel instructed Ahmed to print off police 8 inch by 10 inch head-and-shoulder photographs of Lee Wong from the NPC for ID purposes. It seemed that the young man was quite a troublemaker. He had had several terms in prison and had the reputation of being a drug-addict, dealer and political tearaway. The photograph showed him to be handsome, swarthy with oriental features, and showed him in a plain white shirt.

Angel had managed to muster DS Gawber, DS Crisp and PC Ahaz for the arrest. They were the only available personnel on his team. They arrived quietly outside the Golden Cockerel on the main Wakefield Road out of Bromersley in two unmarked cars. They parked on double yellow lines right outside the recently converted, lofty, Georgian built, Methodist chapel, which had been bought, disembowelled, converted and decorated most luxuriously, into a ritzy Chinese restaurant, fully licensed, and staffed mostly by Chinese. It was owned and run by Mr Harry Wong, the father of Lee Wong.

Angel sent DS Crisp and PC Ahaz to the rear of the building where he assumed there would be a kitchen or staff access, while he and DS Gawber climbed the stone steps to the large front entrance. They pushed open the heavily varnished door into the lushly carpeted reception area and were greeted by a beautiful Chinese lady.

'Table for two, sir?' she enquired.

Angel smiled . . . man's natural response to a pretty female face.

'No, miss. We're from the police. We're looking for Mr Lee Wong.'

She courteously lowered her head, revealing her undulating jet-black coiffure, and looked to one side. It was the cue for a

27

middle-aged, slim Chinese man to step forward. He was dressed in a suit as clean and as sharp as a Hatton Garden diamond.

'I am Harry Wong,' the smooth, monotonous, unvarying voice said confidently. 'Can I be of service, gentlemen?'

The Chinese lady drifted smoothly away.

Angel knew Harry Wong was the proprietor of the restaurant and also owner of a wholesale business that supplied foodstuffs, equipment and all the requirements of the specialist Chinese food-catering business to other Chinese. He had heard that Wong also loaned money to some members of the Chinese community to set up their own businesses; there had been rumours however that his interest rates were very high.

Angel pulled out his warrant card and showed it to him.

'I'm looking for your son, Lee, Mr Wong.'

Wong's lips tightened, then quickly relaxed. He peered at Angel's warrant card most carefully.

'I see. He's not here, Inspector Angel. He has been gone a week.'

Angel pocketed the warrant card, sniffed, rubbed his chin and cast his eyes around the restaurant.

'Where is he now?'

Wong put up a hand.

'I wish I knew, Inspector. I wish I knew.'

'Do you mind if we take a look round?'

Wong shrugged. But didn't reply. He seemed not to object.

'You have rooms upstairs?' Angel said.

'I live upstairs with my wife. We have a flat. My son has rooms up there also. Would you like to start there?'

Angel nodded.

'May as well, Mr Wong.'

'Please follow me.'

He led the way through the restaurant.

Angel noticed how clean and airy the place was. The eighty tables were lined up symmetrically, with glittering glassware and shining cutlery on crisp white cloths each set for four persons. Along one side of the room was a long bar with twenty tall stools in front of it; two smartly dressed men stood smartly behind it awaiting customers. Six huge and brilliant crystal chandeliers hung from the ceiling, each having fifty or so candle-shaped white lights. A dozen or so tables had customers seated at them, waiting or being served by busy, clean-looking uniformed young men and women.

Wong waited silently at the bottom of a wide oak staircase for Angel and Gawber, then politely indicated with a straight hand to them to precede him.

At that moment, Angel spotted DS Crisp and PC Ahaz come through a serving-door used by waiters. Crisp shook his head. Angel nodded knowingly and indicated to him to look around the other offices and rooms on the ground floor. But he was already convinced that, because Wong was co-operating so willingly, there was not a snowball in hell's chance of them finding Lee Wong on the premises that afternoon.

Angel and Gawber trudged up many steps to the top of the building and through a door that Wong unlocked with a key on a chain from his pocket. They were introduced to Mrs Wong. Angel thought she was a delightful lady and he guessed she had probably been a Hong Kong beauty queen not that many years ago. She courteously showed them around the six-roomed flat and then the two rooms allotted to their son. The policemen opened all wardrobes and cupboards that might have been large enough to conceal a man and discovered nothing. Everywhere was smart, clean, minimal but, most significantly, there was no sign of Lee Wong, nor any indication of his having been there recently.

When, at length, all possible places of concealment had been explored, Mr Wong suggested that they sat on the easy-chairs facing the big window that looked out over

30

the rooftops of Bromersley town and at the excellent view of the town hall clock. Mrs Wong invited Gawber and Angel to have a cup of tea, which they declined, so she joined her husband on the plush settee.

'You see, Inspector. You should have believed me. I do not know where my son is. He left here a week ago, before the fire at that MP's home in Mantelborough. The police from there also came round, and, like you, they searched the place. They suspected him because of his past involvement in the drug business and his political views. They had a warrant for his arrest . . . I suppose you have.'

Angel nodded.

'Your son has a dreadful record, Mr Wong,' Angel said quietly. 'Only out of a prison a month and two MP's houses fired . . . after threats that he would bring this government down.'

'I swear to you, Inspector, that my son has had nothing to do with these fires.' Wong spoke quietly and earnestly. 'I know he has been in trouble with this drugs business, and indeed he's been addicted, but he's clear of all that, now. He has been through a resettlement programme in prison. He is drug free. He has abandoned his old life. He is not in touch with any groups in London any more. He has settled down up here with his mother and me. There is a home and a job for him here. He has no reason to go back to his old life.'

Angel was unrelenting.

'You should tell *him*, Mr Wong. Not *me*.'

'We have had very meaningful discussions, my son and I, and he has given me his word that he has nothing to do with these arson attacks.'

'So you keep saying, Mr Wong, but the fact is, he makes threats and the fires keep happening and your son is not here to defend himself, he is not here providing alibis so that we could exclude him. In view of his past record, his drug-dealing and his association with the Freedom party, what am I to believe?'

Wong shook his head wearily.

Angel said: 'Why don't you tell me where he is? Save us all a lot of time and trouble.'

'I'm half out of my mind with worry, Inspector. How can I convince you? I simply have no idea where he is. He told me that prison was the most devastating time of his life and he has no intention of ever returning there. He is afraid that some over-zealous politician or policeman might create a case against him and he'll finish up inside again, and he simply couldn't bear that. That's why he's hiding, Inspector. Believe me. I know my own son.'

Mrs Wong was seated next to her husband. She was holding his hand and earnestly nodded her agreement with every word.

Angel might have become persuaded of Harry Wong's honesty, but not quite. He took a business card out of his pocket and offered it him.

'Mr Wong, my phone number is on there. If your son turns up or contacts you, will you let me know?'

Wong took the card and looked at it. He licked his lips.

'Yes, if he agrees, Inspector . . . if I can persuade him.'

Angel shook his head.

'If he is innocent, Mr Wong, he has nothing to fear.'

★ ★ ★

'Anything at all, Crisp?'

'No, sir. And we had a good look round the kitchen. We looked in the pantry and also went into the deep-freeze. Nothing. The outside extends through into some Atcost buildings, where they store tons of rice and the veg and more cold rooms for meats and whatever.'

33

'No signs of Lee Wong?'

'None, sir.'

The phone rang.

He reached out for it. 'Angel.'

It was the civilian telephonist on the main switchboard.

'Inspector, there's a strange woman,' she said stuffily. 'A Mrs Buller-Price wants to speak to you.'

'There's nothing *strange* about Mrs Buller-Price,' he said sharply. He didn't want his callers psychoanalysed and vetted by the woman on the switchboard. 'She's an old lady,' he insisted tersely. 'Please put her through at once.'

The telephonist wasn't pleased.

Mrs Buller-Price was a genteel elderly widow who ran a small dairy farm single-handedly on a rather desolate and hilly part of the eastern slopes of the Pennines, which was one mile from Tunistone village and cattle and sheep-market and five miles from Bromersley. Angel had known her many years and held her in great respect. She was scrupulously honest, rather odd, but he had become used to her eccentricities over the years. She also made the most wonderful Battenburg cake.

There was a loud click that made a deliberately penalizing uncomfortable echo in his ear, then he heard her familiar educated voice.

'Is that Inspector Angel?'

'Yes. Now then, Mrs Buller-Price. What is the matter? Are you all right?'

'How nice to hear you, Inspector. No, I am not all right. I have been in some great pain with my back, a pain that would not go away. Dr Lemon has prescribed some wonderful new painkillers, so now I am a lot better. But I do admit, I am a little upset. I don't want to bother you with it, but I don't know whom to ask.'

'What is it, Mrs Buller-Price? I will help if I can.'

'Ah, well now. You know I had a beautiful black cat called Tulip?'

Angel sighed.

'No. I can't say that I knew that,' he said gently.

He was familiar with her menagerie of five dogs which followed her everywhere and greeted him rather too enthusiastically on his rare visits to the farm. Indeed, she had taken the occasional ill-treated dog from police custody up to Tunistone farm and given it a very good life. But he was not familiar with her having a liaison with any cats.

'Ah, well,' she continued. 'Tulip was a cat given to me by Princess Michael of Kent. She

35

had been given it by somebody who had thought she had said that she had a mouse in her apartments in London. However, she said that she couldn't look after him properly so would I like him, and I agreed. I have had him more than six years now. He has the run of the farm, but he sleeps in the stables and keeps the mouse population in order, you know. I think that he is about eleven years old. He's the most beautiful cat you have ever seen. He has one of those Gourmet meals every day of his life and almost half a pint of Jersey milk from Buttercup.'

Angel shook his head and rubbed his chin.

'Yes, and he's . . . gone missing.'

'Oh yes,' she exploded. 'How ever did you know? Has somebody brought him in?'

'No. I just . . . guessed. No. Nobody has brought him in. You really want the RSPCA, you know, Mrs Buller-Price.'

'Oh dear.'

'Never mind. I will report it. When did he go missing? And how would you describe him?'

'Yes, well, thank you. He went missing a week ago. Well, he's all black . . . jet black, beautiful yellow eyes, he's big, male, of course. And answers to the name of 'Tulip'.'

'Leave it with me, Mrs Buller-Price. I'll report it officially and I'll ask around.'

She thanked him profusely and invited him, as she always did, to come around for tea and partake of some of her baking. He thanked her, hoped that her back pain would soon ease, replaced the phone and rubbed his chin.

'Tulip!'

Crisp was stifling a smile.

Angel noticed. He gave him the paper with the notes on it.

'Here,' he growled. 'It's all there. Report this to the RSPCA. Lost near Tunistone. And ask them to come back to me if it turns up.'

Crisp grinned.

'Right, sir.'

He closed the door.

Angel scratched his head.

'A black cat?'

He was still wondering whether a black cat was supposed to be lucky or not when the phone rang. He reached out for it.

'Angel.'

It was Superintendent Harker.

'Job for you,' he snapped. 'Suspicious death. Woman's body found in a house at Bottom Bank. Number thirteen.'

'Thirteen?' Angel said, his voice up an octave.

'Are you deaf, lad? Aye. Thirteen. Found by a postman, who made a triple nine. Asquith

37

has sent a car down with a PC. Wrap it up quickly, lad. We've a lot on.'

There was a click and the phone went dead.

Angel sniffed and pressed the cradle on the phone to clear the line. Black cat. Number thirteen. All he needed was a pointed hat and a broomstick.

He dialled the CID room; PC Ahaz answered.

'Ahmed, there's a suspicious death reported down at thirteen Bottom Bank. I want you to tell SOCOs DS Taylor, and also Dr Mac and DS Gawber and DS Crisp, and ask them to meet me there, ASAP.'

3

Thirteen Bottom Bank was the last little Victorian cottage at the end of a terrace on a country lane on the outskirts of Bromersley. It had originally been built for members of the gardening staff of the nearby country mansion Branksby Hall, which was about a mile away. The mansion had long since been converted into a college, which taught computer studies and other modern subjects to mature students.

As Angel turned into the lane, he saw a police car parked out on the road and the SOCOs' white van in the drive. He pulled up behind the car, went through the little front gate and up to the PC on the door. He was pleased to see that it was John Weightman, a big man, old for a PC, who was well-liked and coming up to his retirement.

'What's this then, John?'

'Good afternoon, sir. It's a woman ... Wilde's her name ... on the kitchen floor. In a pool of blood. Not a pretty sight.'

Angel wrinkled his nose. He thought he knew the name. He wondered whether it was the glamour queen he had last seen at the auction on Saturday afternoon . . . buying that hideous doll.

'Is it Imelda Wilde?' he said to the big man.

Weightman's eyebrows went up knowingly. He nodded.

Angel reckoned that Weightman must have heard the gossip. He glanced round the small front garden and said, 'Who found her?'

'Postman. He has gone on with his round. Says he'll call on his way back. I've got his name and address.'

He nodded.

A SOCO in a white paper suit, hat and pink rubber boots came out of the front door unrolling POLICE DO NOT CROSS tape and tying it around trellis-work.

Angel turned to him.

'Any sign of a weapon, lad . . . indication of cause of death?'

'Couldn't see anything, sir.'

'Dr Mac arrived?'

'He's with the body now, sir.'

'I'll be in . . . in a minute. Get me some whites and gloves.'

'Right, sir.'

The SOCO went back inside.

Angel heard a vehicle's brakes. He looked towards the lane. It was the postman. Angel watched him get out of the little van and come through the front gate. He took in his

40

appearance. He was in his early twenties, had a big nose, big ears, dark hair, Elvis Presley sideburns and no hat. As he made his way up the path, Angel saw him look downwards, cover his mouth with a hand and begin to rub his cheeks repeatedly in a nervous massaging action. When he was nearer he saw that his face was flushed, his eyes watery and he was breathing irregularly.

Angel took a step forward to meet him.

'Are you all right, lad?' he said, thought-fully.

The man shook his head. 'It'll never be the same again . . . coming here, to this house, up this path,' he said wiping his lips with a handkerchief. 'Yes. I'll be all right . . . in a bit.'

'You found Mrs Wilde, and rang in?'

'Yes,' he said. 'I always thought this van-run would be a doddle, you know. Out in the country. Better than any town 'walk' . . . but I never expected anything like this. And she was ever so nice.'

The young man eventually removed his hand from his face, put his hands on his hips and breathed deeply several times. Then he wiped his eyes with his sleeve.

Angel pursed his lips. He took his time.

'I'm Detective Inspector Angel. What's your name?'

41

'Sean Putnam . . . I shouldn't have gone in, I know that now . . . but the door was ajar. I shouted several times. Got no reply. You see, I had a package . . . she had to sign for . . . I missed her with it on Saturday. She must have been out. So I took it back to the office.'

'What happened this morning?'

'The door was open. I mean actually ajar. Only two or three inches . . . I called out. I said, 'It's only me . . . it's the postman, Sean. I've got a packet for you to sign for. Are you there?' Then I pushed it further open and called in again. I knew that she lived on her own. You see she doesn't like me to leave a card for her to come to the general to collect it. I did that once and she didn't like it.'

Angel nodded.

'There was no reply, of course. So I pushed the door open even further and then I saw a foot . . . through the table-legs. It had a stocking on it, but no shoe. Then further up, the other foot . . . with a silver sandal on it . . . at a queer angle. She often wore those sandals, so I knew it was her. She was in the corner . . . squashed between the wall and the sideboard. I went straight in. I thought she might have fallen or something . . . then I saw it . . . blood . . . in a little pool running on the lino under the table . . . and she was like a bundle of rags with arms and legs and hair

'. . . it was awful . . . '

His head and his arms were beginning to shake as he remembered the scene. He was working himself up into a state.

'All right, Sean,' Angel said quietly, gripping his arm.

'You see, I've never seen a dead body before.'

'Did you see anybody around . . . just leaving or . . . ?'

'No. I didn't see anybody. I know there are stories going around about her . . . but I never saw anything.'

Angel rubbed his chin.

'What sort of stories, Sean?'

There was a pause. Angel took his hand away from his arm and waited. Sean looked up. He was regaining his equilibrium.

'I don't know,' he lied.

'What stories?'

'Nothing, really. Just rumours,' he said and sighed.

Angel stared at him.

'What rumours?'

'Just what people say,' he replied, shaking his head. 'Personally, I don't believe a word of it. It's just that she's such a good-looker. And always so friendly.'

'What rumours?'

Angel stared at him, insistent on a reply.

'I don't know.' Sean Putnam wriggled his shoulders awkwardly.

Angel maintained the stare in silence.

'You know . . . that she would go with you. You know, for money and that,' he said with an embarrassed snort.

Angel wrinkled his nose.

'Did she offer to go with *you* . . . for money?' Angel said

Putnam sniggered, looked to each side, down at his feet then he came up grinning. When he saw that Angel was serious and that his face was set like the Rock of Gibraltar, he stopped grinning, resumed the staid expression and said firmly, 'Oh no. *No.*'

Angel reckoned that Imelda Wilde had made a compelling impression on this young man; she would have been able to manipulate him round her little finger.

'You're on this delivery run regularly?'

'Mostly. For two years. Ever since I started working for the post office. They change us around sometimes.'

'Did she get many packages to sign for?'

'About one a week, I think.'

'Where is the package you needed a signature for?'

'It's in the van. Do you want to see it?'

'I'll take it. I'll sign for it . . . on behalf of the police, of course.'

44

'Well, I suppose that's all right, yes. Sure. OK.'

Angel heard the sound of vehicle engines. He looked round and saw two cars pull up behind the Royal Mail van. He could see that the drivers were DS Gawber and DS Crisp.

Angel had extracted all the information he needed from Sean Putnam at that point, so he had the postman drop the package intended for Imelda Wilde into an EVI-DENCE bag, which he signed for and stuffed into his pocket. Then he thanked the young man for his assistance and told him he would need a statement from him at a later time.

Sean Putnam forced a nervous smile, then scurried away from the scene as fast as his black boots and the little mail van would carry him.

Angel sent Crisp along the lane on a door-to-door, while he and Gawber changed into sterile paper suits, headcoverings, boots and gloves and went through the front door into the sitting-room of the small cottage.

It was pleasantly furnished and clean.

The SOCOs had not wasted any time. The stairs and the bedrooms were already covered over with plastic sheeting. One of the men was on his hands and knees with a hand vacuum in the sitting-room, systematically traversing the floor.

Angel and Gawber crossed to the door into the tiny back kitchen. Squashed behind the sitting-room door, between the table and the kitchen cupboard, was the body of Imelda Wilde. A beam of a powerful white light mounted on a tripod was directed on to it. A SOCO photographer flashed and clicked away at all angles of the body, the kitchen and the back door. He seemed to be finishing off as Angel and Gawber entered. A few more flashes and he went out.

The pathologist Dr Mac, a small, white-haired Glaswegian who was an old friend of Inspector Angel, was kneeling at the side of the huddled remains. He was checking a stand thermometer to record the ambient temperature, when he heard them squat down next to him.

'Hi Mac, what you got,' Angel said quietly.

The Scotsman grunted.

'This your case, Michael? Not much yet. Nasty,' he observed softly.

Angel moved closer and peered over his shoulder. He looked at the rumpled body: her black hair was irregularly stained and matted in streaks with blood, producing a burgundy colour. The front of her thin turquoise summer-dress was also soaked with ruddy brown blood that had coagulated. Her long, stocking-clad legs showed just above the knees. Her left leg was straight without any footwear, while the other was bent at the knee and then underneath it in an unnatural position, making the outline of a figure 4. There was a high-heeled, silver sandal on her foot.

Angel turned away.

'I suppose it *is* Imelda Wilde?'

'Yes.'

'Hmmm. What's the cause of death, Mac?'

'Stabbed. Once only. With a short knife. Serrated. Probably a regular kitchen knife.'

Angel and Gawber exchanged glances. They glanced round the little room.

'Any signs of it?'

'No.'

'When do you think it happened?' Angel asked.

Dr Mac rubbed his chin.

'Haven't finished my sums yet, but sometime last night, or early evening, I'm thinking.'

Imelda Wilde seemed to have lived a simple enough life. There were no signs that she shared the place with anyone else . . . no signs of a husband, partner or woman friend.

The back door opened behind them. Angel turned. It was Crisp.

'Got a minute, sir?'

'Aye. I'll come out,' Angel said.

He closed the door and joined Crisp on the crazy-paved path.

'What you got, lad?'

'Nothing much, sir. Nobody saw anything. None of them seems to like her.'

'Why? What's a matter with the lass?'

Crisp smiled, knowingly. 'The woman next door said that when Imelda Wilde came to live here it knocked ten thousand pounds off the value of her house.'

Angel wrinkled his nose.

'Bit of a snob, is she? Did you find out what she did for a living?'

'Yes, sir. She was a sort of housekeeper or something to Fred Butcher. He lives in some converted outbuildings, stables in the grounds of Branksby Hall. It's a college now. It teaches computer studies and stuff.'

'Fred Butcher?' Angel said thoughtfully. 'Name rings a bell. What does he do?'

'He was a magician, sir. On the telly.'

Angel's eyebrows shot up.

'Oh yes, I remember. Mysto,' Angel said animatedly. 'He used to make a girl disappear before your eyes and then she'd reappear in the audience. Fantastic. He was a magician. The best I ever saw. He was marvellous. Not seen him around for years.'

'He's retired, sir,' Crisp said less enthusiastically.

48

Angel nodded.

'Yes. Yes. I suppose he must be.'

Angel looked at him, frowned and then said, 'I want you to check on her phone bill. See who she talked to. And her mobile, if she has one. Then get back to me.'

'Yes, sir,' Crisp said.

Angel knew he must see Fred Butcher while the crime was fresh.

★ ★ ★

'Come in,' Harker yelled.

Angel pushed open the door. Sounded like trouble.

'You wanted to see me?' Angel said, looking down at him at his desk.

The superintendent's face was red and turning purple. He was biting his lip, banging the desk top and waving a sheet of A4 in the air.

'Yes. Yes. Yes!'

Angel closed the door. He could see and hear that he was heated up about something. He wished a course of colonic irrigation on him . . . clear out the toxins and cool him down.

'There's another one of those anonymous threatening letters from Lee Wong,' he stormed. 'This time it's to *our* MP, Martin

Pennyfeather. He's a junior minister or something at the Home Office, you know. A very big wheel. *Now* it's on our own patch. It was bound to happen. It's intolerable. We can't have young thugs threatening our MPs. It's outrageous. Are you sure that Chinese lad isn't hanging round his father's place, trying to hide from us?'

Angel shook his head. 'We gave the place a thorough going over, sir. What's the letter say?'

'I've got a photocopy of it,' he said, throwing it in his general direction. 'He got it this morning in the post. Sent it round.'

It glided around in the air for a second before settling on the desk in front of him. Angel picked it up. It was competently typed on a plain sheet of paper.

It read:

Dear Mr Pennyfeather,

You are the third MP I have written to. The other two chose to ignore me and my organization, and have suffered accordingly. We need you to change your political ideas. We do not want you and yours to continue telling us what to do. We have rights of our own. One of them — the most important — is that we reserve the right to deal with our bodies as we see fit. And if we want to take drugs, it is a matter for us and nobody else. You and your government are continually whittling away at our personal liberty. You politicians will soon do all our thinking for us. You are showering laws down on us like rice at a wedding. Very soon we shall have no original thoughts of our own. It seems that all you want us to do is obey you, go to work, and pay taxes. We shall become like zombies. Soon you will have stolen our minds from us. In some countries, they call it brainwashing. You should ban all the drug laws. If we want to take H or coke or amphetamines, it's up to us. We don't want a nanny state. You rich and powerful people think you can dictate to us, but we won't stand for it. When we are 18, we can vote, we can fight for our country, we should therefore be able to decide whether or not we want to use drugs.

I am giving you plenty of time to demonstrate by your actions in Parliament (so that it will be reported clearly in the papers or on the TV) that you intend doing something constructive to repeal the drug laws.

If I hear and see nothing to indicate that you intend taking this action, by ten a.m. on Thursday morning next, 13 April, I will implement immediate retaliation.

Look out, Mr Pennyfeather. You have been warned.

Yours truly,

A friend.

Angel licked his lips. It certainly was worrying.

'Not much of a friend,' he said thoughtfully. 'This is the *third* letter? Any fingerprints? Any postmark? Anything about the paper or the envelope? Saliva on the gum?'

'SOCO have come up with absolutely nothing,' Harker said, much less frenetically. 'No prints, letters printed on a computer, posted in three different post-boxes in Bromersley, envelopes moistened with tap water, stationery from a supermarket chain.'

Angel nodded.

Harker continued: 'On each of the two previous occasions, a mortar shell was somehow lobbed into the house and landed at the bottom of the stairway in the hall. It burst into flames and in each instance gutted the houses. These are large and very expensive properties, three or more storeys. It is no exaggeration to describe them as mansions. They are not little terraced houses. At the last fire a young woman was carrying a baby of six months across the hall when the incendiary exploded. By some miracle she was able to protect the baby, but the young lady herself, an *au pair* from Holland incidentally, is now in hospital with twenty-five per cent burns. We can't allow this to continue. This young hooligan has to be stopped.'

Angel agreed.

'I want you to take on this case. I want you to make it your number one priority. He has made threats before and has always kept them. In each case, within six hours of the expiry of the deadline, the house of the targeted MP was almost gutted by fire. If that girl dies, it will be manslaughter. Now you have two, nearly three days to find him and stop him from carrying out his threat on this third home.'

Angel's eyebrows shot up. He had three murder cases he was working on and murder had always taken priority over all other categories of law-breaking.

'Me, sir?'

'Yes. *You.* Why? What's the matter, lad? Did you intend having a few days' rest and relaxation on your yacht?'

Angel didn't reply. He didn't appreciate sarcasm.

Then Harker thrust the file of papers that he had hastily assembled into his hands.

'Here, lad. It's all in there,' he said. 'You know what to do with it.'

Angel didn't reply. He knew what he would have liked to do with it, and it would have been painful, required the services of a surgeon and was illegal.

He stormed up the corridor to his office, slammed the door, dropped the file on his desk, sat down and opened it up. It comprised the addresses of the two previously fire-damaged houses, the names and temporary addresses of the MPs and their families, the police and prison record of Lee Wong, photocopies of the two previous anonymous threatening letters, copies of the fire-officer's reports on the damage at the two houses and the details of the incendiary mortar-shell used.

He hastily read the content and it was perfectly obvious to him that the way to prevent a recurrence of the arson attack was to arrest Lee Wong, but he had to find him first. He would have to put the screws on Harry Wong and his wife.

He pulled an envelope out of his pocket and consulted it. Then he lifted the phone and dialled a number.

It was quickly answered by a lady with a low, seductive sing-song voice. 'Good morning, the Golden Cockerel, do you wish to reserve a table?'

Angel thought it was probably the beauty on the door with the expensive coiffure.

'I would like to speak to Mr Harry Wong, please,' he said evenly. 'This is Inspector Angel, Bromersley police.'

'One moment, please,' she replied with more saccharine.

It took only a moment for the lower, monotonous voice to take over the phone.

'Good morning, Inspector. Back so soon? What can I do for you?'

'I am still urgently looking for your son, Mr Wong. Has he turned up or been in contact with you?'

'No. I wish he would ring or contact us. His mother and I are extremely worried. Has there been a development?'

'Yes. I'm afraid there has. I'll have to ask you to come down to the station, urgently.'

Twelve minutes later, Angel hurriedly showed Mr and Mrs Wong into the interview room. They sat next to each other and he and Gawber sat opposite. He showed them the photocopy of the letter that the MP, Martin Pennyfeather, had received in the post that morning. Wong read it carefully, then re-read it and handed it to his wife.

'This is not from my son, Inspector. He doesn't think like this . . . he doesn't talk like this. He'd never write like this.'

Angel shook his head.

'Mr Wong, I have seen him . . . and heard him . . . a few years ago, on the television . . . he was spouting this sort of political claptrap by the yard. I can't say whether he was actually saying what's in this letter, but he was using the sort of language that out-of-office, irresponsible would-be politicians use . . . slogans and catch-phrases and . . . promising easy, popular actions.'

'That was *then*, Inspector. He has changed. Prison's changed him. He is a different person. He broke away from the drug-pushers and the people who had encouraged him. *He* was the one whose liberty had been taken away. *He* was the one deprived of the hard drugs that had been his life since he left university. He got off drugs. He's clean. He's sober. He's a changed man. I wish you could have met him after he was released, Inspector.'

Mrs Wong nodded at every point her husband made.

'This is true, Inspector,' she added earnestly. She had her hand on his arm throughout the interview, sometimes squeezing it, sometimes stroking.

'I wish we could convince you, Inspector,' Wong added.

Angel's mouth tightened.

'Well, why is he not here then, to defend the charges?'

'He has run away because he knows that he will not be believed by you, the police, the authorities, the newspapers. They have never believed anything he has said.'

Angel glanced at Gawber, who sighed, shook his head and looked at his watch.

'Is there any wonder? He had such a terrible record,' Angel bawled. 'If he was here, and he was innocent, he could at least put forward alibis . . . alibis of the times of the launching of the incendiaries . . . *then he could be eliminated.* I'm sorry, Mr Wong . . . and you, Mrs Wong. It must be hard for you. But you have to face up to the facts.'

The Chinese man held his head in his hands and said, 'He is totally innocent. If this threat was removed . . . if he was no longer afraid of the police . . . of going back to prison, I am sure he would come back to us. And be willing to speak to you.'

Angel was no longer listening. He had heard all these sort of excuses before.

'I have to take this threat seriously, Mr Wong,' Angel said. 'The two previous threats *were* carried out. There is every reason to expect this threat will be.'

'It isn't my son,' Wong wailed.

Angel watched the man holding his head

and his wife holding his arm to support him. He considered what they might be going through. Children can give their parents so much grief. They often have no idea of the amount of pain they put them through.

He sniffed. He mustn't start going soft on them. He consciously tightened his lips.

'Let's have a five-minute break,' he suggested. He got to his feet, looked across the table. Mrs Wong's sad eyes and appreciative expression complemented her physical beauty.

'Tea?' he said.

Mrs Wong forced a smile and nodded.

'That would be very nice, Inspector.'

Angel switched off the recording-tape and went out of the interview room to the CID office to find Ahmed. He told him to take two cups of tea into the Wongs and then to stay with them.

4

Angel and Gawber went down to the corridor to the vending-machine and furnished themselves with plastic cups of tea.

After a sip Angel turned to Gawber.

'Well, Ron, what do you think?'

Gawber wrinkled his nose. 'You can't tell.'

Angel nodded.

'If they're acting, I'd give them an Oscar. They're not overdoing it.'

He slurped more of the tea, then tightened his lips.

'I hope we're not missing anything.'

Gawber glanced at him.

'We've no other suspects, sir. What else can we do? I can understand the lad keeping away from us. With his record and reputation for trouble, it's understandable. If he walked in here and gave himself up, we wouldn't believe a word he said, until we had checked it out.'

Angel nodded. It was true.

'Wong senior said that he was certain that his son would come home if we dropped the charges against him,' Angel said rubbing his chin.

'In the meantime, what's he doing for

money? Can't live on fresh air.'

'No. Hiding with friends, relatives? Are they financing him?'

'Has he got a car, his own transport?'

Angel nodded.

'Aye,' he said. 'We're not beaten yet.'

He drained the plastic cup and threw it resolutely in the wastepaper basket.

'Come on,' he muttered.

They returned to the interview room. Angel nodded at Ahmed who went out and closed the door. Angel switched on the recording-tape and took his place at the table as before.

The Wongs looked refreshed and alert.

If you have finished with us, Inspector,' Mr Wong said, 'I'd like to get back. I've a business to run, you know.'

Angel's eyes flashed.

'Finished with you?' he bawled. 'Finished with you? I've only just started, Mr Wong. We have to stop this arson attack your son has threatened. You don't seem to realize how serious this is!'

'I've told you it isn't Lee. It isn't my son Lee who has threatened anything.'

Angel stared across the table at Wong.

'How much money did your son have on him when he ran off?'

'He was hard up, I know. He borrowed a

60

small sum from me and he had his last pay-cheque. He would have . . . four or five hundred pounds at the most.'

'And credit cards.'

'No credit cards. The Wong family do not have credit cards.'

'And does he have any friends . . . relations . . . anybody he could be staying with?'

'He wouldn't be staying with any of the people from his old life. And we have no relatives in the UK. We have relatives . . . my brothers-in-law in Hong Kong, but Lee was born here in Bromersley . . . and has never met them.'

Angel shook his head.

'What sort of car does he drive?'

'He doesn't drive. He had his licence withdrawn for being under the influence . . . '

Angel sighed. 'So you have no idea where your son, Lee, might be hiding out?'

'Sadly, no. And I repeat, Inspector, my son did not set fire those two MP's homes and he has not threatened to set fire to a third. As I believe you say, you are barking up the wrong tree.'

Angel shook his head. He reached into his pocket, pulled out a handkerchief and wiped his forehead. Then he stared unfocused in the general direction of the window while reaching up to rub the lobe of his ear between finger and thumb.

Gawber knew the look. He discreetly pressed his arm down and forward on the table and edged his jacket sleeve back sufficiently to steal a look at the dial of his watch. It showed ten past five. He sighed. He knew he was going to be late for his tea again that day.

Mr and Mrs Wong looked intently into Angel's big, tough face.

At length Angel glared back at them and said: 'You persist in defending your son, which I suppose is understandable, but it defies the evidence. If *he* is not responsible for these arson attacks, who do you suppose is?'

The Wongs looked crestfallen. They turned to each other briefly, then looked across at Angel.

'I have no idea,' Wong said.

Mrs Wong shook her head.

'Could it be someone else who holds the same political attitudes as your son?' Angel suggested.

'It could be, of course, Inspector, but we don't know any of them. That was three years ago when he lived in London.'

Angel turned to Gawber, who looked dismayed. He was thinking what Angel had been thinking. It was a long shot, and it would have been difficult to ascertain who were Lee Wong's principal supporters, aides and so on, to find them, interview them, charge them and lock them all up in two days. Such a task could prove to be more difficult than finding Lee himself.

Angel nodded in agreement to the unspoken understanding with Gawber and turned back to Wong.

'You cannot think of anybody . . . *anybody* who might have a grudge against your son or you?'

'No,' Wong said.

His wife nodded her agreement but then suddenly her face changed. She turned back to her husband and leaned closer to his ear. Angel heard her whisper, 'There's Conrad Sweetman.'

Wong's face stiffened. He looked at her.

'No,' he said firmly.

He shook his head decisively, and put up his hands in objection.

'It could be him,' she said, her beautiful big eyes shining like a tiger's. 'It could be him. He vowed to get his own back, didn't he, Harry? He said he wouldn't rest until he had seen you in hell!'

Wong wrinkled his nose; the corners of his mouth turned down as he thought of the man he hated.

He shook his head several times.

'No. Leave that be, Lily.'

'But it *could* be him, Harry!' Mrs Wong said earnestly.

Angel thought that Wong considered that it was possible that his wife could be right, but that there was something holding him back.

'Tell me about this man, Mrs Wong,' Angel said.

'It is not good, Lily,' Wong said sternly, 'and quite improper to discuss our personal and private business with the Inspector.'

'Well, Harry,' she said gently, putting a hand on his. She began again: 'My darling, this situation is desperate. I am far more interested in the safe return of our son to us, than keeping secret the shabby way Conrad Sweetman treated you all those years ago. We have . . . *you* have nothing to be ashamed of.' Then looking more deeply into his eyes, and with an expression that would have melted most people's hearts and might have deserved a BAFTA, she added: 'Now, either you must tell the Inspector, or I will.'

Wong, unmoved by her appeal, pulled his arm from under her hand, leaned forward across the table, his jaw set square, and his eyes, like two currants, glided from side to side.

Angel waited patiently. He folded his arms.

He hoped the wait would be worth it.

Gawber took another sly peek at his watch. He didn't like what he saw. Mrs Wong looked intently at her husband while fingering her string of expensive Mikimoto pearls.

'Very well,' he began, pursing his lips. 'I suppose it is possible that my wife could be right about this man.'

'Tell me,' Angel said impatiently.

Wong's face looked dark and strained.

'It is certain that he has made plenty of threats against me. I would have preferred to have dealt with him in my own way.'

Angel wondered what he meant. It sounded very ominous. Did he mean getting one of his henchmen to kill him quietly and dispose of him in the River Don?

'About five years ago, as Chinese food became ever more popular in UK, and I was expanding my business rapidly, I needed a reliable, honest man to act as cashier to collect and bank and keep the records of the restaurants and takeaways I owned or in which I had a financial interest. Some paid me an agreed amount, usually monthly, to be collected in the way one might pay a rent collector. It was in that way that some of my Chinese friends were able to repay me the loans that I had made to them to assist them to enter into business for themselves. The repayments were usually informal 'family' arrangements and the restaurateurs or take-away shopkeepers would repay me directly through their takings. Also my wholesale company would supply them with the basic foodstuffs at very advantageous prices. At the beginning I did all the collecting, banking and accounting personally, but it got too much for me, so I advertised for a cashier. I had a reply from a man who had recently retired as a major in the Royal Artillery, was used to handling men and cash and running the finances of a unit of a thousand men.'

'Royal Artillery?'

'That's what he said. Yes. I interviewed him. He was impeccably turned out, smart suit, polished shoes, umbrella, bow tie . . . everything. Very presentable. His references from his CO and from a general could not have been better. So I engaged him. At first everything went well. But quite soon there were some discrepancies. Monies from the shops did not tally with the amounts paid in. Simply, he was fiddling the cash payments and the amounts did not match up. I faced him with it. He challenged the system of arrangements I had with the staff in the shops. He thought I wouldn't prosecute him, but I did. He was sentenced to two years for fraud. Of course he had forged all his references. And as far as I could discover, he had been a crook all his life. Had never been caught, therefore not charged and therefore had no police record until I challenged him. I believe he came out of Armley prison about two months ago.'

'The timing fits,' Gawber whispered.

'There's more, Inspector,' Mrs Wong said excitedly.

Her husband pulled a face.

'This was all most embarrassing, Inspector. Sweetman challenged everything. Everything had to be verified. However an independent auditor introduced by the police confirmed the charge against him. Over twenty thousand pounds. The court hearing was, of course, most embarrassing, Inspector. And it became very personal and vindictive . . . as if in some way I was directly responsible for him committing the crime. It was difficult to know why the man was so personally offensive, when *he* was stealing from *me!*'

'Personality disorder,' Angel said. He had seen it many times.

'After he was sentenced, from the dock he promised revenge on me and my family,' Wong continued. 'He threatened it over and over again. He would not stop repeating the threats. The warders eventually had to drag him down the steps.'

Mrs Wong sighed and smiled wanly at her husband.

Angel looked at Gawber. At last, there was something to get his teeth into.

'Find this Conrad Sweetman.'

★ ★ ★

Michael Angel drove into Bromersley police station yard onto a marked parking space next to the white Ford van with *Gaimster & Gibson, ventilation engineers* painted on the side. He hardly noticed it and fed his card into the rear door-lock of the station; it clicked open and he let himself into the building. He made his way up the corridor and arrived promptly in his office at 8.28 a.m. He dragged off his raincoat, reached out for the phone and dialled a number.

Ahmed Ahaz answered.

'Good morning, sir.'

'Good morning, lad. I want to see DS Crisp in here smartly. And I want to know what SOCOs and Dr Mac have on the Imelda Wilde case. Find out where they're at. And if *you* don't get a helpful response from the SOCOs office, you can tell them *I'll* be straight round with my steel-tipped boots on.'

'Right, sir.'

'And I want a cup of tea, Ahmed. And get me the fire-officer who dealt with the arson attack on the MP's house at Mantelborough. I'll speak to him first.'

'Right, sir.'

Angel put down the phone. It rang immediately. He picked it up again.

'Angel.'

It was Ron Gawber.

The inspector was surprised. 'Yes, Ron?'

'It wasn't difficult finding Conrad Sweetman, sir. He's in a cell at Skiptonthorpe police station. I'm on my way there now.'

Angel's eyes lit up. There was progress already. He hoped it was the right man. Rarely was the finding of an accused as easy as this seemed to be.

Skiptonthorpe was a small town six miles from Bromersley towards Rotherham.

'Interesting. What's he doing in their pokey?'

'Don't know, sir. I'll find out and let you know.'

'While you're there, take his fingerprints. Don't bring copies of theirs. Do it yourself. You haven't forgotten how, have you? Aye, and there's something else. Don't interview him. I don't want him knowing that he's in the frame for arson . . . not just yet. Got it?'

'Right, sir.'

'And bring back a photograph of him. And

make sure it's recent and actually looks like him: I want to know what sort of a monster we're dealing with. And keep me posted,' he finished, and replaced the phone.

He rubbed his hands like a bookie at a January meeting. It was a good start for a Tuesday morning. He glanced at the pile of post in the middle of the desk and was about to riffle through it, when there was a knock on the door.

'Come in.'

It was Crisp.

'I got the info on Imelda Wilde's phone bill,' he said pulling out his notebook. 'She doesn't have a mobile.'

'Are you sure?'

'No, sir. Can't say I'm *sure*, but SOCO says there's no sign of one, and no bills for one, either.'

'She might have a pay as you go.'

Crisp nodded.

'She might, sir. The phone itself could even have been taken by her murderer. If there was something in it that he might want to conceal.'

Angel nodded.

'Well, whom did she phone?' he said tetchily.

'Shops and butchers and hairdressers. No regular calls apart from Fred Butcher. She rang him about three times a week. They didn't seem to talk long . . . '

Angel said: 'Fred Butcher. Mysto, the magician. Anything known?'

Crisp frowned.

'Don't know, sir.'

'Well find out, lad, and let me know. What's his address?'

'He lives in some outbuildings of Branksby Hall that are part of that adult college, up the road from where Imelda Wilde lived.'

'Right, lad,' he said, pulling an envelope out of his pocket and scribbling a note on the back of it.

'And she phoned Max Starr's theatrical agency in Leeds, on Friday last. All her other calls seemed to be shops or businesses. Nothing out of the ordinary.'

'Get me this Max Starr's address. And see if we've anything on *him*.'

'Right, sir,' he said and went out.

Angel watched the door close, then shook his head. He rubbed his chin and glanced at the pile of post in the middle of the desk and was about to riffle through it again, when there was another knock on the door.

'Come in.'

It was Ahmed, carrying a tin tray with a beaker balanced precariously in the middle of it.

71

'There's Chief Fire-Officer Metcalfe on the line, sir. He's the man who was in charge at the fire at Mantelborough.'

'Right,' Angel said, taking the tea in one hand and picking up the phone with the other.

'Good morning, Chief Metcalfe,' he said into the mouthpiece, then took a trial sip of the tea.

Ahmed went out and closed the door.

'And good morning to you, Inspector. What can I do for you?'

'You had a nasty fire at the home of Sir Hector Tippington, at Mantelborough, last Tuesday . . . arson, they said?'

'Yes. Arson, it was. Very bad indeed. The house almost a total loss. Over a million pounds worth of damage. Still, no loss of life, that's the main thing.'

'Yes. Quite. Well, what can you tell me about it, Chief? What started it?'

'I heard there was another, night before last, wasn't there, similar, round your way?' Metcalfe sniggered.

Angel's lips tightened.

'Yes,' he replied grudgingly. 'Fred Charles-worth. MP for Beston North.'

'Another big country pile,' Metcalfe said. 'Your arsonist only picks on big houses. Leaving the smaller fry alone. Your local

Bromersley station will be able to fill you in on that, Inspector.'

'Yes, I'll get round to them. Please tell me about your blaze. There's a girl in hospital badly burned.'

'Yes there is. An *au pair*. Bad show.'

'What started it?'

'A small incendiary bomb, sixteen inches long, weighing six pounds, ten and a half ounces. It's known as a BZ2. The sort of thing that used to be dropped in their thousands from the air. In this instance, it must have been fired through a window from some sort of mortar.'

Angel pursed his lips, then blew out a foot of breath. He thought that incendiaries and mortars were only used in wartime.

'A mortar?'

'Yes. A lightweight tripod thing. Not heavy. One man could carry it. Would need a rigid base to set the feet in, though.'

'Wouldn't work on a pavement or road?'

'Probably not. Might do. It would . . . slide around . . . the recoil on those things, you know.'

'How about mounted on the back of a vehicle . . . so that the arsonist could make a quick getaway?'

'Possible. Bolted down. It would need to be something substantial. I don't think you could set up a mortar on a car and then fire it with any accuracy. Would need to be something sturdy . . . back of a heavy lorry or similar . . . maybe.'

'Could it have been fired from a garden, say?'

'Oh yes. I suppose you could dig it in. Need a man with experience to set it up and aim it. You'd need to get the trajectory right, of course. Bomb disposal . . . Or ex-army man with artillery experience would know.'

Angel nodded. He knew just the man and he was currently behind bars in Skiptonthorpe nick.

He had all the information he needed. He finished the conversation politely and replaced the phone.

He finished the tea, then rang Ahmed.

'Where's DS Crisp?'

'He isn't in CID and I couldn't raise him on his mobile, sir.'

Angel made a noise like a hungry bear.

'When he turns up tell him I want to see him,' he growled.

'Yes, sir.'

'Now get me Martin Pennyfeather's telephone number. He's our MP. Lives in a big house on Elmsworth Road.'

'Yes. Right. I know it, sir,' Ahmed said.

He replaced the phone.

Angel reached over to the pile of envelopes, reports and general mishmash that constituted his daily tedium of paperwork. He began to finger his way through it, trying quickly to work out the sender of each missive and then, without opening it, guess at its contents. The motive was to save time by dealing only with the urgent and important communications. Some of the time, the system worked and he could save an abundance of time: unfortunately guesswork was not one hundred per cent accurate!

The phone rang again. He reached out for it.

It was the woman on the station telephone reception. There was another call from Mrs Buller-Price. Angel pulled a face. It was a not a very convenient moment. But he had a soft spot for the old lady and would always make time for her.

'Put her through,' he heard himself say.

There was a click.

'Good morning, Mrs Buller-Price. Now, how is your back today, feeling better, I hope?'

'Ah, dear Inspector Angel. Good morning to you. My back is still painful, but a lot better, thank you. Dr Lemon has given me some wonderful new pills. However, I am sorry to bother you again, but really there is such a lot happening here that I think you should know about.'

'My dear Mrs Buller-Price, if it is criminal, then I certainly *do* want to know about it. That's what I am here for.'

'Ah, well, now, this first matter *is* criminal. It is a case of trespass. And damage. Now you know that in addition to this farm and the field around it, I own Lucifer's Patch, the zed-shaped field higher up where the ruins of that monastery are, and where I sometimes, in the spring, let my little herd munch off some of the spring grass?'

She stopped talking. Angel felt obliged to say something. He had no idea what she owned or what she let her cows do.

'Well, yes,' he said, to keep the story going.

'Yes, well, yesterday afternoon, I was in the bathroom . . . standing on the stool, my back didn't care for that, I can tell you . . . looking through my telescope and I distinctly saw something . . . in silhouette on the horizon, in the ruins between the surviving pillars of the monastery, a large black shape . . . with things sticking out and hanging off it. I thought it must be a converted bus or caravan of sorts, probably inhabited by a family of gypsies. Or travellers of some sort. Anyway, it was very large and I felt quite disturbed by it. So later on, while I was steaming a kipper for

76

my tea . . . I do so love kippers . . . I can remember when I could eat two! Tulip adored kippers. I always used to give him a bit, and he loved the golden brown skin. I don't suppose you've heard from the NSPCC or whatever they call themselves these days . . . about him? Have you?'

'No, not yet,' Angel replied patiently. 'But I had not forgotten about him.'

'Oh, thank you, Inspector,' she replied warmly. 'Now where was I? Oh yes. The trespasser. After tea, I decided I would take the dogs for a walk up there, find out who was in the wagon, and ask them to leave . . . you get all sorts of queer and unsavoury people . . . Schwarzenegger is a great guard-dog you know. He wouldn't have let anything happen to me.'

'And what happened?'

'Well, I cleared the table, put my new leather walking-boots on . . . and we trudged up, the six of us. When we got there, the vehicle had gone!'

'Oh,' he responded with a low sigh.

'Yes. I had a look round and noticed the fencing had been damaged . . . about twelve feet of pig-wire had been driven over. Also, the top gate had been left pulled to, but not latched. So I latched it, but I can't repair fencing now. That sort of work is past me.

With my back. I'll have to get a man out there . . . cost me at least a ton of Pipers to put that right. It's trespassing, you know, Inspector. Trespassing. I wouldn't mind so much if they didn't do any damage, but invariably they do.'

'Yes,' Angel said. He didn't like anonymous travellers on his patch, who materialized in daylight, in nondescript transport, and parked up unlawfully. Inevitably they were dishonest, or mischievous and disappeared into the night. 'I'll get someone to take a look, Mrs Buller-Price, when I can. In the meantime, if the trespasser returns, let me know at once, and I'll try and organize immediate police presence to investigate him and take him in or send him on his way.'

'That's indeed very kind.'

'Now you said there were other things happening up there . . . ?'

'Yes, there are, Inspector. Very odd. Now you know me, I'm not easily afraid or unnerved. I've lived up here on my own ever since my dear husband died. But, I have to confess I am getting really quite nervous. You see, somebody . . . it may be a child or somebody . . . or something . . . has been in my house several times this past week. I haven't actually seen them. But my small frying-pan has disappeared . . . the one I fry my bacon in every morning. I normally keep it on the oven top . . . at the back. Well, that went missing on Sunday. On Monday, yesterday, the spare key to the stable, which I keep on a little hook by the fireplace, went.'

'Oh? And what's in the stable?'

'A rather old saddle and some tack, Inspector. Nothing more. Whoever wants it can have it. I shall not ride any more. And this morning, I was doing some baking . . . I had need to go in the pantry for a new, unopened three-pound bag of white flour, and that had gone! The whole bag. I don't know what's happening, Inspector. Since my back-trouble, it's as if someone has put a curse on me.'

'Is the house ever left unlocked?'

'Only when I am out milking. I never thought I had need to lock it up when I go round to the barn. But that's what I'm doing now, Inspector. Odd that the dogs don't seem to hear or notice . . . a stranger about the place.'

'I'll come round to see you as soon as ever I can, Mrs Buller-Price. I promise you. In the meantime, always keep your door locked.'

'I certainly will. And you can come for tea. You're always welcome, you know that. Any day. I have the kettle on at a quarter past three. And I have just baked a batch of scones. You'll love them, absolutely weighed down with fruit. And I will look forward to seeing you again soon. Thank you, Inspector. I really must sit down now, my back is killing me. Goodbye.'

He replaced the phone.

He rubbed his chin. It was very worrying to hear that an intruder had actually entered Mrs Buller-Price's house. She was an old lady living on her own, miles from anywhere. And the pain in her back could be very debilitating. He considered that the thefts were much more serious than the trespass on her land. An intruder had actually entered her house . . . several times, apparently. Yet the items taken were not what a conventional thief would be interested in . . . they hadn't much value. The loss of the items was more of an inconvenience than anything else. He knew that the farmhouse had many items a thief might consider valuable . . . silver items and antique bits galore . . . the table cutlery, the tea-service, barometer, French bracket-clock, grandfather clock . . . What thief worth his salt would want to steal a used frying-pan, a stable key and a three-pound bag of flour? It didn't make sense. It was another of those annoying conundrums that would come to the surface of his mind whenever he was thinking about nothing in particular.

He was determined to get up to the farm and investigate the situation very soon. He reassured himself briefly when he considered that if her brindle Alsatian dog, Schwarzenegger (whom he knew from old) had sunk his molars into a prowler, that unwelcome visitor would certainly require medical attention ... an anti-tetanus jab at the very least, and he wouldn't forget that in a hurry. However, the old lady shouldn't have to depend on a dog to be safe in her own home in this day and age.

He sighed heavily.

He knew there were evil people around Bromersley at this present time. In addition to the invasion of Mrs Buller-Price's home and land, there had been a gruesome murder of a most beautiful woman, Imelda Wilde, down at 13 Bottom Bank, and an arsonist threatening to burn down the home of Martin Pennyfeather and his family.

Angel was not a happy man.

5

He turned the car off Elsworth Road, through the big iron gates and then pointed the bonnet down the long drive to the big, three-storey, detached stone house, set in its own grounds. He turned right across the gravel, throwing up a spray of the stuff and making a swishing sound, and stopped opposite the six stone steps leading to the door. He made the steps, eyed the porcelain-centred shiny brass bell-push and applied his finger to it. The heavy door was soon opened by a slim lady with protruding teeth and a big smile.

'Good morning,' she said, showing the full thirty-two. 'You must be Inspector Angel. Please come in, I'm Primrose Pennyfeather. You *must* call me Primrose . . . *everybody* does. My husband is expecting you. Please come this way.'

She held out a hand and shook Angel's firmly. He reciprocated and, in doing so caught a look in her eye that made him think that behind the welcome, the manners, the *bonhomie* and charm was a frightened woman desperately putting on a show of composure; she had probably been directed at her rich mother's knee always to smile and look at ease even in times of great danger. And this was such an occasion.

'Pleased to meet you, er . . . Primrose.'

He followed her into the large entrance hall which was dominated by a big oak table in the centre. There was a pile of letters and packets on one corner of it. Two red-and-yellow children's bicycles were leaning incongruously against it. On the left was a wide impressive staircase, leading up to the two or three floors above, and at the far end, some banisters at the head of steps that led down to the basement. The floor and the wood-work gleamed with years of polish and everywhere smelled of beeswax and money.

She closed the front door and crossed the hall to the door on the right of it.

'He's in here,' she said, flashing the teeth again.

It was a drawing-room with many chintzy upholstered chairs and settees. A baby grand piano occupied most of the bay window; the oak-panelled walls were liberally covered with large gilt-framed oil-paintings of important-looking men in knee-breeches with children and dogs around their feet.

Angel looked round the big room for the man he was to meet.

'This is Inspector Angel, Martin,' she called

out to her husband.

'Thank you, darling,' he called.

He spotted Pennyfeather. He was sitting by the fire-place, partly concealed by the wing of a chair, and holding up, arms outstretched, a copy of a pink newspaper.

The door closed.

He lowered the paper.

'Come in, Inspector. Come over here. Please sit down.'

'Thank you,' said Angel, and selected a comfortable chair opposite the man.

'I hope you have some good news for me. It's about time the police were showing some concern for the victims of this arsonist, and reeling the hoodlum in.'

There was a distinct touch of ice and lemon in his voice.

'We are doing our best, sir.'

Pennyfeather sniffed.

'Two houses have been burned out without the police taking any notice or instituting any preventative measures . . . or offering any protection against this Chinese hooligan. Have you caught him yet, this Lee Wong . . . and slapped him behind bars?'

'No. Not yet, sir. It may, of course, not be him.'

'Of course it's him. What other political lunatic would be running up and down lobbing incendiary bombs at people's houses. I hope you are going to afford my family and my home protection from this madman. He has been successful twice before. The trouble with you people was that you didn't take the threats seriously.'

Angel had to agree that that might well be true, but the police could not possibly respond to every anonymous letter, and the demands and the threat in these instances were so outrageous, they seemed to be the work of a crank.

'Well I'm certainly taking this threat seriously, sir. You can rely on that,' he said very firmly. 'The deadline given by the arsonist is 10 a.m. on Thursday morning. Now, at a quarter to ten this house will be surrounded by policeman, and two patrol cars will be circulating around the perimeter. You can be assured that you and your family will be adequately protected from any possible attack. Nobody will be able to get in or out of the place. It will be as tightly contained as a tin of pilchards.'

'I do hope so.'

'How many people live here?'

'My wife, myself, and our two children. We have three part-time staff, but none of them lives in. While this threat is hanging over us, I am sending my wife and our children to stay with her sister in Rotherham. My wife is putting some things together now; they will leave this afternoon.'

'Good idea. Now over the past week or so, have you had any visitors or workmen or strangers visiting the house? Anybody you cannot vouch for?'

'Certainly not.'

'You've had no alterations made to the house recently?'

'No, Inspector. None at all.'

'Now, your staff: can they be entirely trusted? How long have you known them?'

'My constituency secretary, Mrs Joyce Peel, is the latest to come to work for me. Comes from an impeccable family. Been with me about six months now. Hargreaves sees to the outside, the garden and so on. Been here many years, fifteen or more, ever since we moved in. And Mrs Hargreaves, his wife, runs the house, she's the housekeeper. Salt of the earth . . . don't know what we'd do without them.'

Angel nodded and noted their names.

'Tomorrow I will send a team to search the house . . . check that everything is safe and that there is nothing abnormal or dangerous . . .'

'Whatever for? What would you be looking for?'

'You want us to be thorough, don't you?'
The man sighed.

Angel said: 'To tell the truth, I don't know what to look for. But we don't want to miss anything. I'll want to check out every room and every cupboard inside the house and every garage, summerhouse, shed and building outside. We'll search the garden and the grounds . . . any place big enough to conceal a person.'

★ ★ ★

'*How many?*' the superintendent roared.

'It'll take twenty-four uniformed men at least, sir,' Angel said.

'Twenty-four? Don't be ridiculous. Where do you think Asquith is going to be able to scrape up twenty-four uniformed officers from?'

Angel continued, undeterred.

'My team will be responsible for searching the house and the grounds. And I also want two marked cars for high-profile patrol around the perimeter.'

Harker's nose was the size and shape of a Victorian brass bath-tap; he wrinkled it, which was not a pleasant sight.

'Can't allocate that sort of numbers to a *threatened* arson, lad. I mean, it isn't as if

Wong could actually execute this half-baked threat a *third* time . . . not when he knows we are on to him. The papers have been full of him and this business. He'll not come out of the wood-work again . . . not when he can see what forces he's up against.'

'It might *not* be him, sir.'

Harker blinked.

'It must be. You're not seriously considering it could be this chap, Sweetman, are you?'

'Conrad Sweetman?' Angel shrugged. 'Not sure, sir.'

'Ah, but that's invention. It's just an old dispute conjured up by Wong's father to try and get his son out of the frame, that's all. It's merely a delaying tactic. It's an old trick.'

'I'm trying to keep an open mind,' Angel said evenly. 'The arsonist could set up a mortar near the grounds and somehow project the incendiary through a window into the house. Sweetman was in the Royal Artillery, he'd know about things like that.'

'Ridiculous,' Harker sneered. 'Would require some projection and delicate precision aiming-mechanism. And there would need to be sufficient momentum to be sure the missile would detonate on impact. And the mortar itself, that would inevitably be highly visible in the grounds or the street. And the arsonist

88

would need to be as precise as a brain surgeon. And he would only get one shot at it. Anyway Sweetman's in Skiptonthorpe nick, isn't he?'

'He might not be there on Thursday, sir. I'm waiting to see what Gawber has found out. Whoever is the arsonist, he has done it twice before . . . and the houses were gutted. I have noted that the Mantelborough fire was started six hours and a quarter after the ultimatum expired, and the Beston North fire, six and three-quarter hours after that ultimatum ran out. I don't understand why there is a thirty-minute difference . . . only the arsonist knows that. Anyway, if we were to take an average, then the likely time of the attack on Pennyfeather's would be . . . six and a half hours after the ultimatum . . . that's . . . 16.30 hours on Thursday.'

'Hmmm,' the superintendent snorted looking at his watch. 'Plenty of time. That gives you fifty-two hours to find Lee Wong and get him locked up.'

★   ★   ★

'Come in,' Angel called.

It was Crisp.

'What do you want, lad? I'm up to my eyes in this arson thing.'

'It's about Fred Butcher, Mysto the magic-man.'

'Ah yes,' Angel nodded and pointed to the chair. He must keep up with everything.

Crisp sat down.

'I've been on NPC and there's nothing known. I've been asking around. Everybody gives him a good name. You know, sir, I remember seeing him on the telly when I was young. Made an elephant disappear. He was very good. Well, I thought so at the time. And you also asked me to look up Max Starr, theatrical agent, Leeds. He comes out clean also. I've got his office address. Been established in Leeds about fifty years . . . been at the same address thirty.'

Angel rubbed his chin.

'Must get to see both Butcher and Starr . . . leave them to me, and don't sniff around them. Don't arouse their suspicions.'

'Right, sir.'

'Now, tomorrow, I want you to chase round SOCO and see what they've got. Ask Don Taylor. Also, if they've finished, you can get access into Imelda Wilde's place. In particular, I want to see any letters, address book, photographs, bank statements. You know what I'm looking for. Contacts. Male contacts. She's been murdered by a man . . . with an evil temper.'

'Sure it's a man, sir?'

'Pretty well. If it was female, I wouldn't want to meet her on a dark night.'

Crisp knew what he meant. It would be *some* monster. He nodded in agreement.

'Crack on with that. On Thursday, all day, you'll be with me at Pennyfeather's place.'

There was a knock on the door.

'Come in.'

It was Gawber.

Angel smiled.

'You're back. Come in, Ron. How did you get on?'

Gawber's shining eyes indicated success. He smiled as he pulled some photographs out of his inside pocket and placed them on the desk in front of Angel.

Crisp made for the door.

'Hang on, lad, Angel said. 'Come and look at these. This is one of the suspects.'

Crisp peered over his shoulder.

'There,' Gawber said and pointed to three colour photographs. '*That*'s Conrad Sweetman. Face, front and profile, and full length. I had a job on to get him to stand up for *that* one. He's a difficult . . . difficult man.'

Angel looked at the photographs. They showed a short, smart, clean-shaven man with tidy hair, in a suit with shirt and red bow tie.

Gawber pulled his notebook out and read from it: 'He's forty years of age, five feet four inches tall, weighs nine stones twelve pounds. Unmarried. Bachelor. Lives on his own. No known associates.'

'He looks . . . just like a . . . dapper businessman. Bachelor . . . not interested in girls? What's the matter with him? Is he interested in the other, then?'

'Nothing known about his private life, sir. He speaks with no particular accent. He was a bit woozy. Needed a shave.'

Angel glared at him.

'You didn't interview him, I hope?'

'Oh no, sir,' Gawber said.

Angel nodded.

'What do you mean, he was woozy, Ron?' Crisp asked.

'He was drunk . . . or drugged. Drunk, I expect. You could smell brandy on him.'

Angel frowned. He rubbed his chin.

'Really?' he said, and shook his head. It didn't seem in keeping for an arsonist to be smelling of alcohol.

'The fingerprints match?'

'Yes, sir. It's the same man. I've checked.'

'Positively the same man that fiddled Harry Wong back in 2001 and went to Armley jail for it?'

'Yes, sir.'

Angel squeezed the lobe of his ear between finger and thumb. 'And what's he doing locked up in Skiptonthorpe?'

Gawber smiled and shook his head.

'Drunk and disorderly. Found sitting on some empty market-stalls in the main street, waving an umbrella and noisily haranguing passers by. Apparently he likes his bottle, does Conrad Sweetman. He's been inside for similar charges a few times lately . . . the desk sergeant told me. He's not very popular at *that* station: when he's had a skinful, he sings all night.'

'Better get times and dates,' Angel said.

'Right, sir. He'll be in front of the magistrates about now. By the look of him they'll keep him locked up at least until he's sober, until late this afternoon.'

'Did you get his address?'

'Yes sir.' He pulled his notebook out of his pocket. 'He lives at 36 Park Street, Bromersley.'

Angel pulled a face. That was significant topography.

'That's not far from Martin Pennyfeather's place!' Crisp said.

Angel added: 'You could walk it in three minutes.'

'But a lot further from Sir Hector Tippington's and Fred Charlesworth's houses, sir,' Gawber said.

'Aye.' He had to agree that that was a fact.

'It's a coincidence,' Crisp suggested.

'A damned convenient coincidence,' Angel growled. 'You know I don't believe in coincidences.'

The phone rang.

Crisp thought it a good time to break away and see if he could get clearance from SOCO to get into Imelda Wilde's house and begin a systematic search through her personal papers and effects.

'I'll get started, sir,' he said quickly and made for the door.

Angel nodded.

'Yes, lad. Thursday morning. First thing. Here,' he replied as he reached out for the phone.

Crisp went out.

'Angel.'

It was Superintendent Harker.

'Now lad, you'll be pleased to hear that I've got twenty-four uniformed and two patrol cars available to you from 9 a.m. Thursday. Asquith's been digging them out from everywhere. The gods must have been looking favourably down on you, lad,' he said grandly. 'It'll be *your* show. But I warn you, you're going to have to catch the bastard to justify all this cost and organization.'

Angel tried to think of something confident

to reply, but he couldn't.

'Yes, right, sir.'

'How are you getting on with the search for Lee Wong?' Harker said pointedly.

He wasn't. Every policeman and woman and every newspaper in the country had been notified. There had even been an appeal on the television, but to date, no sightings had been reported. There was nothing positive he could say to him.

'There have been no responses to our enquiries yet, sir.'

Harker must have been furious. Angel heard him suck in air.

'*I know that*,' the superintendent bawled impatiently. 'I want to know what *new* initiatives you have instigated?'

Angel hadn't instigated any. He had to think quickly.

'I'm going to go back to Harry Wong and see if I can twist his arm . . . see if I can get any more out of him.'

'You'll not get anything more out of *him*. They don't call them inscrutable for nowt, you know. I regret to say that your naïvety is showing, lad. You'd better get your finger out and think of something fast,' Harker banged down the phone.

Angel's lips tightened. He placed the handset back in the cradle.

Gawber looked at him. He knew he had taken a bit of a roasting. He was thinking of something supportive to say.

Angel rubbed the lobe of his ear between his finger and thumb and then turned to Gawber. 'Are you in the mood for a spot of breaking and entering, lad?'

The sergeant looked at him strangely. 'Where, sir?' he said. 'Harry Wong's place?'

'No. Conrad Sweetman's house.'

* * *

Angel parked on Sheffield Road and the two men walked round the corner on to Park Street. They checked on the house-numbers. Number 36 was an even number, so they had to cross the road.

'I don't like this breaking in, sir,' Gawber muttered out of the side of his mouth.

'Sweetman's safely locked up in Skiptonthorpe nick; he lives on his own; there'll be nobody there. This is an ideal time. What are you worrying about?'

'Why can't we simply get a warrant?'

Angel's eyes flashed. He blew out a lungful. 'You don't *have* to assist me, lad, if it's going to worry you. I can manage on my own. You can wait in the car.'

They walked on. Gawber didn't reply.

96

Angel said: 'We can't get a warrant because I don't think the super would approve. It's better to do this 'unofficially' than be denied permission 'officially', if you see what I mean.'

Gawber gave him a blank look and shook his head.

They walked on, checking off the house-numbers on the gates as they passed.

'Did you bring the camera?'

'Yes, sir. What are we looking for, anyway?'

A lady walking a small dog on a lead was coming towards them. When they were level, she peered at them strangely.

Gawber looked away. Angel switched on one of his celebrated smirks, which people who didn't know him believed to be a smile, and said, 'Good afternoon.'

She nodded and cheerily reciprocated.

They walked on some more, then Angel said: 'We'll be looking for evidence, lad. What do you think? Anything that ties him in with the anonymous letters, the political stuff, the incendiaries, the arson . . . '

'You definitely think he is the arsonist, then?'

Angel didn't reply. It wasn't necessary. His mind was on the house-numbers. They were almost outside number 34 Park Street and the property they were interested in was next door, number 36. It was a small, pleasant semi-detached house. He opened the neat wooden gate and walked between it and number 38 to the back door of number 36. Gawber followed, quietly closing the gate behind them.

Angel didn't waste any time. He looked closely at the keyhole, sniffed, then pulled a box of skeleton keys out of his pocket, chalked up a blank, inserted it in the keyhole and began the tedious process of picking the lock.

Meanwhile Gawber looked round to see if they could be observed by anybody. The small back garden contained a few evergreen bushes planted around a rectangle of adequately maintained turf, which some people might call 'the lawn', beyond that were more houses. By the back door was a black rubbish-bin on wheels. He lifted the lid expectantly and discovered it was empty. It was a disappointment. There were frequently some useful clues in and amongst the rubbish.

There was a click and Angel withdrew the two picks.

They were in.

He pushed open the door and Gawber followed.

The house was small, pleasant, airy, and

clean and tidy throughout, and was furnished with typical traditionalist furniture with a leaning towards minimalism in line with a bachelor's pad in the second millennium.

There was nothing helpful to their mission on the ground floor . . . simply the usual domestic offices, with furniture and knick-knacks for the basic needs of warmth and sustenance. They moved upstairs. The front bedroom had the traditional bedroom suite with nothing unusual in the chest of drawers or the wardrobe. However, there was a disturbing surprise to come. As they moved on to the small landing they heard a muffled sound of something or somebody moving in the other bedroom.

The noise startled them. They had naturally assumed they were alone in the house. Angel's pulse began to thump and his face and chest were burning. Gawber's eyes opened wide and the backs of his hands had turned to gooseflesh. They didn't speak: they didn't hesitate. With a nod from Angel, although they were unarmed, together they rushed through the door into the little room and looked round for an intruder. They had expected to see a human or even an animal, but there was nothing alive in the room. However, what they *did* see made them stop and stare in silence.

Above them, suspended from the ceiling by their handles, were a number of, at first glance, about a dozen umbrellas . . . yes, perfectly ordinary black umbrellas in the closed state, just as if they had been standing in a hallstand. They were all the same and apparently symmetrically arranged about a metre apart from each other, although the pattern was not easy to determine. Also, on the bare floorboards underneath were six others in no symmetrical pattern at all, in fact they lay there in an apparently higgledy-piggledy heap.

The two policemen looked from the strange, orderly but incongruous sight on the bedroom ceiling to the less orderly and equally incongruous array on the floor.

'They're umbrellas, sir,' Gawber said.

'Aye, lad. I can see that. Hanging down. But what for?'

Gawber stared up at the ceiling, mesmerized.

'Looks like they've been stuck up there . . . in some way . . . by their handles.'

'Aye, but *what for*?' Angel said, gawping at them and shaking his head.

Gawber didn't hear him. He was so amazed at the sight. His eyes eventually travelled from the ceiling on to the plain, clean, papered walls down to the skirting-board, and began counting. ' . . . four, five, six. There are six more umbrellas on the floor, sir. All the same size, colour, style. Is it all right if I pick one up, do you suppose? Do you think it's safe?'

Angel took his hand from his chin and reached down for an umbrella from the floor. 'I've got one here, lad. Feels all right. Nice ivory handle. No, it's *imitation* ivory, plastic, but it feels all right. A bit heavier than normal, I think.'

He made to open it.

Gawber looked worried.

'What you doing?'

'Opening it. Why not?'

Gawber hesitated.

'Bad luck, sir.'

Angel wrinkled his nose. 'Don't believe in all that rubbish.'

He opened it up, and a spray of small, white particles spewed around the room and over the two men like confetti at a wedding, much to their surprise.

'What's that, sir?'

'Came out of the brolly. Don't know,' Angel replied. He picked off a few particles that had landed in the crease of his coat-sleeve. 'Looks like rice.'

'It might be poisonous, sir. One of those strange chemicals.'

Gawber found a grain on his coat-sleeve.

101

He picked it up rolled it between finger and thumb, then put it to his nose and sniffed it.

Angel put the grains he had found into his mouth.

'Careful, sir. You don't know what it is.'

Angel bit into them and rubbed them on the roof of his mouth with his tongue. 'Yes. It's simply rice. Harmless. The sort of stuff your mother made a pudding from. About a cupful.'

Gawber looked absolutely flabbergasted. 'But what's it doing inside a brolly?'

Angel looked equally bewildered. He shook his head.

'What do you make of it, sir?' he said, staring up at the ceiling.

'I've never seen anything like it . . . twelve of them . . . all closed up . . . hanging up there . . . about a yard from each other . . . filled with rice . . . hanging down from the ceiling . . . whatever for?' He looked down at the floor and said, 'Aye, and six more . . . identical . . . also stuffed with rice . . . apparently thrown haphazardly . . . on the floor . . . it doesn't make sense.'

'In this upstairs room . . . in this house . . . is it to dry the rice, do you think?'

Angel pursed his lips.

'No. Expensive way to do it, I would have thought. In any case, it *is* dry.'

He looked at Gawber and said, 'That sound we heard . . . must have been one of these brollies falling and landing on the floor.'

'Yes. Must have been, sir. There's nothing else in here,' Gawber said pensively, unable to turn his eyes away from the bizarre spectacle. 'Look, sir. The fallen brollies have left a pattern on the ceiling in the shape of the letter 'S'. Do you think that's significant?'

Angel gawped up at the suspended umbrellas. He had no idea. He shook his head, then shrugged. 'Don't know, lad. I simply don't know.'

S for Sweetman?

Then he leaned over and reached out for another umbrella from the floor.

Gawber scratched his head and said, 'Is it a witch's sign or . . . a ritual sign or something like that, sir?'

Angel shook his head. Gawber could see that he was unusually stuck for words.

'No, lad. No. Anyway, it would be warlock, wouldn't it? Sweetman being male? And you mean like three balls outside a pawnbroker's shop?' he replied, then his face changed. He looked up. Thoughtful. His eyes widened, zoomed in on Gawber then closed slightly, his mouth opened a little. He remained like that for a few seconds, then the thought dissolved.

'No, lad. No.'

Angel was not yet ready to give any credence to witchcraft or warlocks or things that go bump in the night.

He thought Gawber was edging that way.

Still crouching, Angel leaned forward and picked one of the umbrellas up from the floor. He opened it slightly to see if it contained any rice. It did. He nodded approvingly and closed it up. 'I shall take this with me. Somewhere down the line, I think that this will prove to be vital evidence.'

6

They walked back to the car without speaking.

Angel held the closed umbrella in his right hand and used it like a walking-stick.

'Nothing about the anonymous letters, the political stuff, the incendiaries, the arson, sir,' Gawber said as he fastened the seat-belt. 'There's nothing there at all that supports a case against Sweetman, is there?'

Angel released the hand-brake and let in the clutch. He didn't reply. He was clearly not in a talkative mood. His mind was in turmoil. The searching of Conrad Sweetman's house had certainly failed to reveal any evidence that he was the arsonist, but Angel had, reluctantly and unwillingly, now become the slave to a mystery . . . a mystery that would surface to the front of his mind every time he tried to rest. From that time onwards, his mind would not be allowed an idle, casual, relaxing moment until he had discovered why a drunken man had suspended from the ceiling in an incomprehensible symmetrical pattern in a bedroom of his small semi-detached house in a respectable part of the

South Yorkshire town of Bromersley, twelve closed umbrellas containing dry plain, white rice.

There had to be a logical explanation for it, and it wouldn't be trivial. It would be for some very evil purpose known only to Sweetman . . . and Angel doubted that the man, if questioned, would be willing voluntarily to give an explanation.

He turned the corner into Church Street to the station; it had been a silent journey; both men were deep in thought. Angel reckoned that you could go all over the world and never see a sight like the one that he had just seen. Even his wide and varied experience had not prepared him for such an unusual spectacle.

Outside the front door of the station, the white Ford *Gaimster & Gibson, ventilation engineers* van was parked up. Angel stopped his BMW behind it.

'Get out here, Ron. Find out where and when Sweetman has been these past few days; set up a timetable of his movements. Start with Skiptonthorpe nick.'

'Right, sir.'

'And there's something else that's making me think, lad. The two houses these MPs lived in were huge mansions, worth a lot of moolah. The property market is on the up. I wonder what they were insured for and what awards the insurance companies are going to shell out. Also, I wonder how much Martin Pennyfeather's place is insured for, with contents: it'll be a pretty penny. There won't be many insurance companies handling that sort of business. Might be a broker specializing in insurance for MPs . . . offering them a special rate. See what you can find out.'

'Right, sir,' Gawber said and slammed the door.

Angel let in the clutch. Three minutes later he was outside Harry Wong's glitzy restaurant, the Golden Cockerel.

He locked the car, ran up the steps and through the big doors. After he had been met by the beautiful hostess, a worried Wong quickly appeared and showed Angel into a small office near the main door.

'Have you some news, Inspector,' Wong said, his hands clenched in front of him and stooping slightly. 'About Lee?'

'No. Nothing. I was hopeful that *you* could tell me something. Have you heard nothing at all since he left a week ago?'

'It's *eight* days now, Inspector. Eight days. Lily is crazy with worry. She is impossible to reason with. No news from Lee is awful, and the accusations of arson and the threat of another hanging over the other MP too, is burdensome.'

'Would you not expect your son to have been in touch with you by now, particularly if he is totally innocent, as you keep on insisting?'

'I think he is too afraid. If he phoned I think he would now expect the phone to be bugged and that he might be traced.'

'Do you still think he is in this country?'

'I do, but I have no way of knowing for certain.'

'And you still believe he is innocent?'

'Yes, of course. But I have no way of proving it. Have you been able to find Conrad Sweetman? The more I think about it, I really do believe he is the man behind these arson attacks.'

'I have traced him. He is at this moment locked up in a police cell.'

'Ah! The best place for him. I congratulate you, Inspector. That was quick work. Is he here, in Bromersley?'

Angel hesitated.

'You understand, I wouldn't want to say exactly where he is.'

'You must keep him there until after the deadline of the arson threat is over.'

'That would be the ideal situation, Mr Wong. And I will certainly do all I can. In the meantime, it would also be helpful . . . extremely helpful if your son was to surrender himself up to us. If he was also in custody . . . in his case, protective custody, I should feel a lot happier about the situation. It might also prove that he wasn't the arsonist and everybody would be happy.'

Wong shook his bowed head. 'Not possible, I regret to say, Inspector. I think I can truly say that as long as you seek my son for these crimes, the more he will hide. However, if he hears . . . *when* he hears that you have charged someone with them, he will immediately return to his mother and me. And that is the day I look forward to, Inspector.'

There was suddenly a noise at the door.

Angel and Wong looked round.

The door was thrown open. It swung back on its hinges and banged noisily on the corner of a stationery cabinet.

Two big men, with oriental features, smartly dressed, burst in. They looked menacingly at Angel, their eyes lowered, their lips curled and their fists clenched.

Wong's lips tightened. He straightened his shoulders, put his hands down to his sides and glared back at them.

'What you want?' he snarled.

They looked at the small man, and one of them said, 'Are you all right, boss?'

'Get out, you imbeciles,' Wong shouted with surprising venom. 'I tell you if I need you. Get back to tables.'

The men's faces changed. Their eyes flashed and their jaws dropped. They looked at each other, then quickly scrambled back to the door, where they stopped, turned round and, looking directly at Angel, the first man said, 'Sorry, sir.'

'Yes, sorry, sir,' the other echoed.

'Get out!' Wong yelled, waving an arm.

The door closed quickly behind them.

Wong put his hand to his forehead, shielding his eyes and massaging his temple.

Angel blew a silent whistle. He was glad they had gone. They looked as if they could have been dangerous if Wong had not been there.

'I apologize for the interruption,' Wong said wearily. He looked up. 'They are two enthusiastic young men. Eager to please. They are at present serving at table here. I am teaching them the business from the bottom . . . where I started. Their loyalty must have got out of hand. Margarita, the young woman I have on reception, may have told them that you were a police officer. They must have misunderstood and thought I may have needed some . . . assistance or protection from you. Please excuse them, Inspector. Their relationship with the police and the police's behaviour in their own country may have coloured their view of the behaviour of police here in the UK.'

Angel frowned. He was thinking what powerful young bulls they appeared to be. Unrestrained, they could really have done him some damage.

'No harm done, Mr Wong. I must go. But if you hear from your son, you must let me know, and you must tell him that if he wants the police to believe that he is not the arsonist, he must report to us and provide the appropriate alibis. There is still time to give himself up before the deadline of the threat to Pennyfeather's mansion, which runs out at ten o'clock, Thursday morning, day after tomorrow.'

Wong bowed his head slightly.

'Good afternoon, Inspector.'

★   ★   ★

Angel's office door opened and Superintendent Harker, wearing a brown trilby and fawn raincoat, bustled in. Angel stood up.

'I'm off,' Harker began, fastening up the raincoat buttons as he spoke. 'Got a meeting at the town hall. Just called in to see what progress you have made finding Lee Wong?'

Angel was surprised at the visit. It was unusual for the superintendent to come up to his office. It showed his great personal interest. Of course it *was* the town's MP's home that was under threat and Harker had very good reason for keeping on the right side of the local town hierarchy, and would no doubt have liked to have delivered the news to the town hall that the man regarded as the number one suspect in the burning down of the town's MP's home was securely under lock and key.

'None, sir,' was Angel's weak reply.

Harker's big ginger eyebrows shot upwards.

'Well what are you doing about it, lad?' he bawled. 'You haven't got long. The clock's ticking you know.'

Angel knew that only too well; he nodded and sighed. He was stumped for something useful to reply.

'I've been to see Wong again. See if his son had showed up . . . '

Harker sniffed.

'Let me guess. I bet he said 'no', and that he hadn't heard a word from him.'

Angel couldn't do anything but stand there and take it.

'You'll have to do summat, lad. Pull summat out of the hat. I suppose you're chasing this chap Sweetman,' Harker said with a smirk. 'You've bought the idea from old Wong that *he*'s the one you want. Well, good luck with it. I only hope you get young Lee locked up before ten o'clock on Thursday or we're going to have another mighty inferno on our hands.'

The door slammed.

Angel sat down, sighed and rubbed his chin.

Harker had perfected the art of making him both angry and uncomfortable at the same time. Nobody could succeed more quickly or more certainly than he could.

Angel was considering what to do next. He closed his eyes and eased himself back in the chair, tilting it so that he was facing the ceiling. He stayed there a few moments, trying to work out what more he could do, but it didn't help any. He eased forward, which brought him down to face the pile of post in the middle of the desk. He opened his eyes, reached out and riffled pointlessly through it; he had no serious intention of settling into any paperwork at that time. His thoughts were on the threat that hung over Martin Pennyfeather and his house, and he was desperately thinking how he could discover the whereabouts of Lee Wong.

The usual quiet of the administrative area of the station was suddenly disturbed by loud and uncouth shouting. Angel was used to disturbances from a drunken or unruly customer in the station occasionally. It was to be expected. This racket came from the corridor right outside his office door and it persisted. He pushed back his chair and leaped towards the door. He yanked it open to see a PC walking a man in handcuffs down the corridor towards the cells. Every two or three steps, the man stopped and the PC had to push, cajole and persuade the man to move forward.

The man was yelling, 'You can't do this to me! I haven't done nothing! Call this justice? I tell you I haven't done nothing. You're not taking any notice of me, Plod. I tell you I haven't done nothing.'

Angel followed them. He recognized the prisoner. It was Harry Hull, small-time house- and shop-breaker, pickpocket, twister and crook, being taken to the cells by PC Scrivens a young constable in his twenties.

Angel frowned, then said quietly: 'What a musical voice you have, Harry.'

'Who the 'ell's that?' Hull said, more raucously than ever, while struggling to turn round.

'Come on, Harry,' the young constable said persuasively and pushed him by the arm.

'Who have you got there, Scrivens,' Angel called. 'Aled Jones?'

'Very bloody funny,' Hull said as he

managed to twist round briefly and see that it was Angel following them down the corridor.

'Oh, it's you,' he sneered. 'Fatty Angel. The great detective,' he added sarcastically and then laughed loudly at his own impudence. 'Fatty Angel,' he said and roared again.

Angel smiled wryly.

They reached the cell block.

Hull quietened down, no doubt subdued by the sight of the steel cell doors.

Angel waited outside.

Scrivens led Hull in, took off the handcuffs, locked him up in cell number one, chalked his name on the board and came out.

'What's he in for?' Angel asked.

'Caught trying to sell a stolen book in the Feathers Hotel sir, the property of Mr Jamieson, owner of The Old Curiosity Shop.'

Angel frowned. 'What sort of a book is a crook like Harry Hull interested in?'

'Apparently a very valuable book, sir,' Scrivens said impressively.

'What? Antique? Out of print? First edition? What?'

'Yes, sir. It's a grimoire, dated 1646.'

'And what's a grimoire?'

'A book of spells, sir.' He referred to the clipboard. 'It's full title is *Dowdeswell's Book of Magick Spells*.'

'Really?'

'He needn't have hawked it round the pubs, sir,' Scrivens said. 'Old Mysto, the magician, Fred Butcher, would have given him a good price for it.'

Angel's mouth dropped open.

* * *

Michael Angel drove the BMW through the gates of the Bromersley police car park as the white Ford van with *Gaimster & Gibson, ventilation engineers* painted on the side drove out. He hardly noticed it as he let himself into the building. He made his way up the corridor and arrived promptly in his office at 8.28 a.m. He stuffed the umbrella he had taken from Sweetman's bedroom between the green-painted wall and a silver-painted radiator pipe that was located directly behind his swivel-chair. In that position, it was safe, handy and upright, and no grains of rice could spill out. He had rather taken to that umbrella, and had decided that he would not be parted from it until he had solved the case and would have to hand it in to the CPS.

He threw off his coat, picked up the phone and dialled a number.

'Good morning,' he said evenly. 'Is that Skiptonthorpe police station?'

116

'Yes. Good morning, sir. How can I help you?'

'This is DI Angel, Bromersley, can I speak to Chief Inspector Whale, please. I take it he is still in charge there.'

'Yes, sir. Yes he is. Hold on. I'm putting you through.'

There was a click and a friendly voice said, 'Good morning, Michael. Well, well, well. Haven't seen you in ages. What you doing with yourself? Still a DI at Bromersley?'

Angel smiled.

'You know I am, Jonah.'

'Is happy, handsome, Horace Caligula Harker still your super?'

'He is. What are you doing with yourself? Still out boozing every night? Why can't you find a nice girl, settle down and get married?'

'Who wants a *nice* girl. I've had too many of *them*. Talking about girls, I hear you're the investigating officer into the death of Imelda Wilde. That should be very interesting.'

'Yes, why?'

'She was a witch, you know. Yes, a white witch. I don't go for all that malarkey myself, but in her case, I'm prepared to make an exception.'

Angel shook his head.

There was a pause. He had no idea that Imelda Wilde was supposed to have been a witch. He didn't know anything about witches and witchcraft . . . but, come to think of it, since the discovery of the body, he *had* noticed little things . . . words . . . references. He wouldn't normally have given witches and witchcraft the slightest thought. But now he had a supposed dead witch on his hands . . . like it or lump it, maybe he would have to give the subject some thought. See if it had a bearing on finding her murderer.

'When you've had a few encounters with the likes of the Rossi family, Jonah, witches and bogeymen don't seem very relevant. Anyway, who says she was a witch?'

'Well known,' he said laughing.

Angel's mind then flew to the strange sight that he'd discovered in Sweetman's back bedroom.

'I don't suppose witches,' he began tentatively, 'black or white are . . . much into umbrellas?'

'Umbrellas, Michael?' Whale whooped laughing. 'No. It's broomsticks they fly around on, isn't it?'

Angel decided not even to mention rice!

'Was Imelda Wilde one of your ex-girlfriends or something?'

'No. I missed out there. Just used to enjoy watching her on a hot summer's day walking or running down Rotherham Road for the bus to town. It was quite a show, more interesting than a pole-dancer . . . Everything moved, Michael. Everything. And the traffic used to slow down. Lightened every man's day. She always wore bright colours. You couldn't miss her. Also, there was a certain mystery about her. I once stood next to her in the post office. When she went in, all the staff behind the tills craned their heads to look at her and hoped she'd come to their window. The women were the same. They were as fascinated as the men. For different reasons, I expect. She smelled different too . . . continental or eastern . . . no idea what it was . . . it was different . . . very potent.'

Angel smiled.

'Sounds like it. I wish I had your imagination, but that's not what I phoned you about.'

'No. No. Expect not. Something uninspiring, I expect. What can I do for you, Michael?'

'You had a visit from Ron Gawber yesterday. He was taking a look at a chappie you have there for me.'

'Oh yes. Conrad Sweetman. Acts like a king. Talks like a lord. Dresses like a barrister: dark suit, spotless shirt, red dickie-bow, polished shoes . . . but he's a real pain in the arse. Drinks all day and sings all night. What's your interest?'

'Is he sober enough to attend court?'

'I expect so. In fact, he's on first. Thank goodness. He'll get a fine and expect he'll be on the streets by five past ten.'

'Ah. Thank you. That's just what I wanted to know.'

'What's your interest?'

'Oh, nothing much. He's possibly in the frame for something else. That's all.'

'Oh. Must be something pretty . . . interesting,' Whale said, his voice rising inquisitively.

'Not really,' Angel lied. 'Thanks very much, Jonah. Keep single.'

'I'll try.'

'Goodbye.'

7

It was ten o' clock.

Angel opened the door of his BMW, turned to Gawber and said, 'You go in the back, Ron. You're getting out first.' Then he handed him the umbrella and added, 'Put that in the back with you. Make sure it stays upright. I don't want rice all over the place.'

Gawber took the umbrella and climbed into the car.

'Ahmed. In the front next to me. Hurry up, lad.'

'Right, sir.'

When the three men were settled and the car doors closed, Angel released the handbrake and let in the clutch for the one-minute journey round the corner.

'Take your hat off, Ahmed. I don't want him spotting us for coppers,' he said as he pulled up on a yellow line twenty-five yards away from the main entrance outside Bromersley Magistrates' court. He switched off the ignition.

Gawber opened the car door to get out.

Angel turned his head.

'Hey, Ron,' he said.

Gawber stopped, looked at him and waited, his hand on the door handle.

'We've only twenty-four hours before the deadline,' Angel said with heavy significance. 'We mustn't lose him.'

'No, sir.'

Gawber didn't need reminding how important this surveillance was. He jumped out of the car and ran through the blue-painted door into the courthouse.

Ahmed pulled out photographs of Conrad Sweetman and began to look at them. He wanted to be able to be certain he would recognize him.

The two men sat in silence for ten minutes.

Angel held his mobile in his hand and watched the big arched blue-painted double doors while tapping the steering-wheel with his thumb. Then the phone rang. He opened the case and pressed the button.

'Yes, Ron?'

'He's recognized me and made a rude gesture. He's made a short phone call and he's paying his fine in the clerk's office. Should be out in a couple of minutes. You'll easily spot him, sir. Medium height . . . wearing a smart, camel-haired overcoat and a brown trilby.'

'Right,' Angel grunted, and kept the phone to his ear.

A few moments later, Gawber said, 'When he comes out, I'll be right behind him. You won't miss him, sir.'

'Better not,' Angel growled.

Suddenly, a local red taxi appeared from nowhere; it raced up to the courthouse entrance, stopped on a double yellow line and stayed there. Its motor was running . . . the regular tick of the diesel engine was audible.

Angel's pulse raced. The taxi completely blocked his previously clear view of the courthouse door. He promptly passed the phone to Ahmed, turned the ignition key of the BMW, and reversed the car ten yards to recover the unrestricted view he had previously had of the courthouse door and steps.

He took back the phone in time to hear Gawber say, 'Coming out now, sir.'

The phone went dead. He pocketed it and both Ahmed and Angel gazed at the courthouse entrance. Sure enough, a short, clean-shaven man in a camel-hair coat and brown trilby hat came out closely followed by Ron Gawber.

Angel stared at him. So that was Conrad Sweetman. Clean, pasty face, expressionless, insignificant. There wasn't much to see despite his stylish clothes.

Gawber was walking immediately behind

him. He didn't glance in their direction. He bounced down the steps on to the pavement and round the corner back to the station.

Sweetman went straight up to the red taxi, got in and it moved swiftly away. Angel started up the BMW and followed it at a discreet distance as it travelled towards Bromersley town centre, past the church and along the main shopping thoroughfare into Victoria Street; it had to slow down in the traffic. It trundled almost to the end of the main street where it pulled up close to the kerb and stopped.

Angel was three cars behind. Sweetman could hardly be at his destination. Angel's pulse increased. He tapped the indicator arm on the control stalk, pulled the front wheels towards the kerb, stopped at a disorderly angle of forty-five degrees, pressed the button that opened the window and waved the traffic on. An angry horn blasted behind him. He ignored it.

Sweetman leapt out of the taxi, crossed the pavement and walked straight through the doors into the Northern Bank.

Angel's eyes were all over the place.

Ahmed watched intently.

'Do you want me to put my raincoat on and follow him in there, sir?'

'No,' Angel grunted. 'Not unless the taxi

drives off. It hasn't moved yet, so I expect it's waiting to take him on somewhere else. He's presumably there to draw out some money. Shouldn't be long. Keep your eye on the bank door. We don't want to lose him.'

A few minutes later Sweetman came straight out of the bank door, across the pavement and into the taxi, which promptly pulled back into the stream of traffic.

Angel swiftly reversed away from the kerb, then followed it, maintaining a discreet distance behind three cars, out of the town centre to the roundabout where the quarry turned off at the third exit on to Sheffield Road. After about a mile, Angel saw the taxi's right indicator lights flash. Sweetman was going into the South Yorkshire retail park. It was a ten-year-old estate comprising many new shops, multiple store branches, independent specialist shops and Cheapo's giant supermarket, the store that sold everything from a pin to an elephant.

Angel sniffed and turned to Ahmed.

'Looks like now he's got money, he's going to spend it.'

Angel slowed the car, tapped the right indicator and drove the BMW into the estate. He changed down to second gear and trundled slowly along until he could see where the taxi was headed.

The taxi pulled up outside the main doors of Cheapo's.

Sweetman got out and the taxi quickly drove off.

Angel found a parking-space nearby with a good view of the main doors.

'Stay here, Ahmed. Keep your mobile handy. When he comes out, let me know.'

Ahmed nodded and dived into his pocket for his phone.

Angel dashed into the store, dodged two pretty girls wearing sashes and brandishing leaflets, grabbed a wire basket and went through the chromium plated barrier into the area where the pins and elephants were supposed to be. He walked purposefully up the huge centre aisle. He knew exactly what he was looking for . . . a short man in a camel-hair coat with a brown hat. He reached the far end of the aisle, turned and came back, systematically checking the thirty or forty aisles to his left and to his right. There were a hundred or so customers in the store: big, small, fat, thin, pleasant, some not so pleasant, some pushing wire trolleys, some not, but no man in a camel-hair coat and brown hat. He repeated the drill. He went to the end of each aisle. Then he walked quickly back carrying the empty wire basket and traversed every aisle of the giant store. Still

126

there was no sign of the man. He did it all over again. Twice. Without success. He looked at his watch: he had been in the store thirty minutes. His stomach felt hollow and cold, his mouth dry, and his face was red and sweaty. He feared he must have lost him. He reached in his pocket for his mobile and tapped in a number from the memory. It was answered instantly.

'Yes, sir,' Ahmed said breathily.

'Has he shown up there?' he asked rapidly.

'No, sir.'

Angel brushed his hand through his hair as he continued to glance at every body who came within eye-shot. 'Are you sure?' he asked unnecessarily. It gave him time to think.

'Yes, sir. Have you lost him, sir?'

'No!' he bawled, then bit his lip. 'Just don't know where he is. He's got to be here somewhere, if he hasn't got past you.'

In the distance, Angel could hear a two-note police-car siren.

'Can you hear that racket, lad? Is it near you?'

'Yes sir.' Ahmed's voice suddenly rose an octave. 'It's just pulling up at the front of the store,' he said incredulously. 'It's uniformed's duty car,' he shrieked.

Angel's lips tightened. 'What the hell are

127

they doing here? They're going to frighten him off,' he bawled.

'There's WPC Baverstock and PC Weightman . . . they're rushing into the store. What do you want me to do?'

Angel's mind was everywhere.

'Nothing,' he said, then quickly added, 'Yes. Keep your eyes peeled for Sweetman,' he snapped and then he cut Ahmed off and rapidly tapped in a button from the phone's memory.

'Communications,' a young man's voice came back through the phone.

'Aye. This is DI Angel. Have you sent somebody to Cheapo's supermarket?'

'Yes, sir. The area car. They reported a shoplifter. The staff are holding him on the premises.'

Angel's eyebrows shot up.

'Oh,' he grunted thoughtfully and rubbed his chin.

A fat girl with a squint in a Cheapo's white-and-yellow coat stared at him strangely as she put wrapped brown sliced loaves in wire baskets on display directly in front of him. She fetched her friend dressed similarly but slimmer and without a squint. They both stared at him as he had been hanging around the bakery section for the past five minutes wittering down the phone. He turned away

128

and walked slowly along the centre aisle, as he spoke . . . he was still toting the wire basket, which was conspicuously empty.

'Was there anything else, sir?' the young man from the communications office said.

'No. Thank you.'

Angel closed the phone and increased his speed down the aisle. He was not a happy man. He understood the presence of the area car, but it didn't explain Sweetman's disappearance. He decided to do a sweep of the store again. He looked round to decide where to begin. Then his mobile rang.

It was Ahmed.

'Have you seen him?' Angel yelled.

A passing woman customer looked at him, frowned disapprovingly and hurriedly pushed her wire shopping-trolley away.

'Yes, sir,' Ahmed said, hardly able to speak with excitement. 'I've been trying to get you . . . '

'Never mind that. Where is he?'

Ahmed gulped. 'They took him away . . . in the area car!'

'Took who away? *Sweetman?*'

'Yes, sir. WPC Baverstock and PC Weightman. Just now. Took him away in handcuffs . . . in the area car.'

★ ★ ★

129

Angel was walking up and down his office like a lion in a cage.

There was a knock at the door. He looked round.

'Come in,' he bawled.

It was WPC Leisha Baverstock.

'You wanted me, sir?' she said sweetly.

She was in her twenties and regarded as the station beauty. She really was very pretty and much admired by the men folk, particularly by DS Crisp. But this morning, in this context, her good looks and femininity made no difference to Angel whatsoever. She could just as well have been Alan Sugar in a skirt.

'Yes. Come in. Close the door. What have you done with Sweetman?' he growled.

'He's in a cell, sir. Charged with shoplifting, and D and D.'

'*What!*' roared Angel.

The roar caused the light fitting on the ceiling to rattle.

She looked up at it in surprise. Angel ignored it. He knew exactly what it was. He stared hard into her face.

'What happened!' he stormed.

She glared back with stony eyes. She didn't like being shouted at.

'Communications took a triple nine call from Cheapo's and put it out on the RT. PC Weightman and I were cruising in the area car, and we volunteered to attend. Communications said that Cheapo's manager had reported that they were holding a noisy and difficult drunk, that he had stolen a half-bottle of brandy and had refused to pay for it, that they would definitely prosecute and would we arrest him and take him away.'

'Yes. So what then?'

'We arrived at the store and found this man sitting on the floor in an interview room, drinking from a bottle, refusing to pay for it and refusing to move.'

Angel rubbed his chin.

'Yes. Then what?'

'He was drunk, sir. When we tried to talk sense to him he was rude and aggressive. He refused to pay for the brandy, said he hadn't enough money on him. He wouldn't co-operate. Wouldn't stand up, wouldn't give his name and address. We searched his pockets. That's how we found out who he was. We had no idea he was under surveillance . . . that you had an interest in him.'

'You've checked him in, haven't you?'

'Yes, sir.'

'And how much of that bottle has he drunk. It was actually a half-bottle, wasn't it?'

'Yes, sir. It was almost empty when PC Weightman took it away from him. He smells like a distillery. Sang all the way in the car back here. Terrible racket.'

'You'd better have the MO take a look at him. We don't want him passing out in the cell.'

'That's been organized, sir.'

'Better check on it. And I want to see his personal effects.'

'They're with the desk sergeant, sir.'

Angel jerked his head towards the door, indicating that she should fetch them.

She went out of the office.

Still standing, Angel picked up the phone and pressed a button.

Ahmed answered.

'Yes, sir.'

'Find DS Gawber and send him in here, pronto.'

He replaced the phone and began walking up and down the office again, his hands clasped behind his back.

A minute of thoughtful silence passed. WPC Baverstock came back through the open door carrying a twelve-inch by eight-inch brown envelope with a hand-written list tacked to it. She passed it over the desk to him and said, 'The MO will call in to examine the prisoner on his way back from his lunch, sir.'

Angel nodded in acknowledgement. He

skimmed rapidly down the list and then went through it again more slowly. Then he looked up and frowned.

'It all looks humdrum and predictable except for one thing,' he said staring into her big blue eyes. 'There's no money. And there are no credit cards. No cheque-book either.'

'He didn't have any cash on him. Not even a ten p piece. The desk sergeant noticed and remarked on it. It's correct, sir.'

Angel didn't like it. He didn't like it one bit. He sucked air in noisily through his teeth. 'Everybody *needs* money or . . . the ability to pay their way.' He shook his head, then added, 'What has happened to it? Dammit, he'd just come out of the bank! He hadn't *bought* anything in the store. He'd helped himself to a bottle of brandy but he hadn't *paid* for it!'

Baverstock said nothing; she had nothing helpful to say.

He wasn't pleased. It was something else that didn't make sense. His lips tightened across his teeth. He rubbed the lobe of his ear between finger and thumb.

The hinges on the open office door squeaked slightly and Gawber appeared. WPC Baverstock turned to look at him. They exchanged friendly nods and smiles.

'Ah, Ron,' Angel said, pleased for him to be

there. 'Uniformed have arrested Sweetman!' he announced loudly.

'Yes, sir. I heard. Ahmed told me.'

'Right, well, maybe you can sort this puzzle out for me.'

He remembered WPC Baverstock was still there. He turned to her.

'Well, thank you very much for your help, Constable,' he said evenly. 'You seem to have done everything correctly and according to the book.'

She was surprised to get thanks and appreciation from him in view of his attitude to her earlier in the interview, but she didn't hold any resentment; in fact, she admired his straightforwardness and reputation for getting things done. He was alleged to be the shrewdest detective on Bromersley force and she admired him for that. She just wished he didn't shout so much.

'Right, sir,' she said with a smile, went out and closed the door.

Angel sat down and pointed at a chair inviting Gawber to sit down opposite him.

'Sweetman paid his fine into court this morning,' Angel began quickly. 'He would have had to pay cash, the clerk wouldn't have taken a cheque from him. He took a taxi from the court, for which he would also have had to pay cash. The driver sailed away merrily at

Cheapos, at the end of the ride, so presumably Sweetman paid him off satisfactorily. By the way, the taxi number was 22. I want you to check up on the driver. On the way, he had called in at the Northern Bank. I saw him go in and come out. But when he was arrested he had no money, no credit cards and no cheque-book on him. Then he took a half-bottle of brandy to top up his alcohol level, when he didn't have any means of paying for it. The question is, before taking the brandy, did he see somebody in Cheapos and give them money, if so, who was it and for what reason? Now, Ron, I need this tying up pronto. It might be critical. They'll have CCTV throughout the store, I expect. And it's less than twenty-four hours to the deadline. With Sweetman now drunk and locked up in a cell, he might need to rejig his plans. Anyway, get right on to it and let me know. It's imperative that you find out what happened to his money: who he paid it to, and for what purpose. Right?'

Gawber nodded.

'Right, sir,' he said. He turned to the door then looked back. 'Excuse me, sir. Are you now saying that Sweetman is responsible for the bombs? Have you got some new evidence?'

'No, Ron. I've no new evidence. And I'm

not saying *that*, at all. I'm simply stating the obvious, that if he is locked up, and he's the arsonist, *he* won't be able to carry out the threat. That's all.'

Gawber frowned.

'What about Lee Wong? He hasn't turned up, has he?'

Angel shook his head and sighed.

'The Wongs are remarkably quiet. I haven't heard a dicky-bird on that front.'

8

'Come in. Come in,' the superintendent barked.

Angel closed the office door. He knew it was trouble. He could tell by the way Harker had bawled down the phone to summon him.

'Times pressing now, lad. You've got this 'manoeuvre' on tomorrow. Have you found that Lee Wong character yet?' Harker said, raising his bushy eyebrows and knowing full well what the answer was going to be.

Angel ran his tongue over his lips. 'No, sir.'

'No?' Harker boomed, feigning surprise like a pantomime villain. 'After all this time. Well, well, well. What lines of enquiry are you working on?'

'The usual, sir. Notified all forty-three forces, all sea and airports, newspapers and TV news stations with photograph and full description of him.'

'No response?'

'Nothing.'

The superintendent sniffed. It was quite a blast. 'I see you've got Sweetman tucked away in cell number one. On charges of shoplifting and D and D. Very convenient. And making an even bigger racket than the Arctic Monkeys.'

'Yes, sir.'

'Well I wouldn't bank on him still being there all day tomorrow. That would be very opportune, wouldn't it? My guess is he'll be in front of the magistrates at ten o'clock and be out of the place by five past. You can't expect the magistrates to accommodate us in any way.'

Angel knew full well that that was probably what would happen. The magistrates had to work strictly to the rules of the court, and they wouldn't have responded helpfully to any pressure from the police.

'I thought you said that Conrad Sweetman was the arsonist,' Harker said slyly.

'I didn't say that, sir.'

'I thought you did, lad. In which case, you could charge him and we could dispense with the business of you trooping round Pennyfeather's thumping great house wasting all that time and manpower.'

'No sir. I don't *know* who the arsonist is. But I do expect an attack to be attempted tomorrow. According to my calculations, at the average of the time taken after the two previous deadlines, of six and a half hours. That would make the attack on Pennyfeather's at 4.30 tomorrow afternoon.'

'But if Wong has run off to Hong Kong or wherever, and Sweetman is unfit to appear and is still locked up, how will it be possible?'

Angel felt his shirt-collar getting tight. He put a hand up to ease it.

'Respectfully, sir, you're suggesting a highly unlikely hypothesis.'

'I don't know, lad. I don't know. If only you could have spent more energy looking for that Chinese lad. You could have arrested him and everybody would have been happy. There's plenty of evidence against him. It would have been a damn sight more sensible than snooping around after that drunken smarty-pants in a dickie-bow,' Harker said shaking his head. Then he looked up, 'Have you interviewed him yet?'

'No, sir. He isn't sober.'

Harker muttered something incomprehensible, then sniffed again. Then he said, 'There's summat else, lad.'

Angel breathed in deeply. He wished there wasn't.

'Have you considered the value of Martin Pennyfeather's home and contents? It's not to be compared with the rabbit-hutch on the New Forest Hill estate that you live in. In confidence, I can tell you, I was having dinner last night at the AGM of the Bromersley Resident's Association with the mayor and the mayoress, and as you know, before he retired, he was chairman of the Bromersley Building Society. Well, the recent arson attacks at the MP's homes at Mantelborough and Breston North, came up and, of course, he knows a thing or two about property. He was talking about the value of houses and their contents and insurance claims, and, understandably, Martin Pennyfeather's name came up. And he said he had heard that the freehold and contents of Pennyfeather's place is insured for two million pounds! What do you think to that, lad? *Two million pounds*.'

Angel shook his head.

'It's a lot more than that, sir. I have been in touch with the Political, Legal and Clerical Assurance company myself. They've emailed a copy of the words of the policy. It is insured for three and a half million, and because Pennyfeather is a member of parliament, he gets a special concession. New for old. In the event of a claim, the company would pay out on a new for old basis. And you know how inflation has affected prices the last twenty years.'

Harker's watery eyes opened wider. He wasn't best pleased. He wasn't going to admit it. He didn't quite know what to say.

'Yes. Yes indeed,' he grunted. 'Right, lad,' he said sourly. 'Well, you'd better carry on.'

He waved him out of his office like a king dismissing a slave. 'I only hope you know what you're doing.'

Angel nodded. That was the one thing, the only thing, they both agreed on.

He was pleased to get away. He went up the corridor to his own office and slumped down in the chair. Behind him, stuffed between the wall and the silver-painted radiator pipe was the umbrella. He swivelled his chair round, reached out for it, keeping it upright so that none of the rice inside spilled out on to the floor. He pulled the middle drawer of his desk out four inches and hung it there by its handle. Then he pushed himself back in the swivel-chair and gazed at it. What secrets could a simple umbrella with a cupful of rice grains inside the folds possibly hide?

After a few moments of chin-rubbing and reflection, he lifted the umbrella out of the drawer by its smooth, polished, imitation ivory handle, unbuttoned the elastic fastener that held it in the closed and wrapped state, and pushed the ferrule down an inch or two so that the umbrella opened part-way. He could see a few grains of rice inside, hanging off the black fabric. He tapped the umbrella and the rice fell and dropped lower down inside the brolly. After a moment, he pulled back the ferrule, closed up the umbrella and wrapped the elastic fastener tightly around on to the tiny button. He stood up and, gripping the umbrella at its waist, held it out in front of him like a drum-major.

There was suddenly a knock at the door.

'Come in,' he called, without looking back.

The door opened, he heard someone enter and the door close.

'Who is it?'

'Me, sir. Ron Gawber.'

The sergeant was just in time to see Angel thrust the umbrella out in front of him and waggle it several times like the pointer on a metronome.

'Won't keep you a moment,' Angel said still staring ahead.

Gawber had worked with the inspector for eight years. He was not a bit surprised at these extraordinary activities. He knew that Angel would take any measure necessary to solve a mystery.

Eventually, Angel wrinkled his nose, slowly lowered his arm and looked round at him.

'Have you a tape-measure in feet and inches in CID, Ron?'

'Yes we have, sir?'

'I want to measure the height of it,' he said, waving the umbrella at him. Then he turned to the radiator and tucked it back behind the pipe.

Gawber made for the door. 'I'll get it for you, sir.'

'No. Do it later.'

Gawber came back. 'Have you worked out what the rice is doing in the brollies, sir? Will we *ever* know?'

Angel pursed his lips.

'We'll know,' he said grimly. 'You can't solve a puzzle until you have sufficient information. There are still some facts not known to us. I assure you when all the facts are known, the explanation will become clear . . . like fog lifting out of a valley. It's inevitable.'

'I hope so, sir.'

Angel nodded confidently.

'You'll see. Now did you find out what happened to Sweetman's money?'

'Not exactly, sir.'

Angel pulled a face.

'That means no. Tell me about it.'

He pointed to a chair and the two men sat opposite each other, the desk between them.

'I phoned Skiptonthorpe nick, sir,' Gawber began quickly, 'and established that Sweetman had a hundred and eighty pounds and eighty-two p in his personal effects when he left there this morning to go to court. I found out that he was fined sixty pounds in total, which he paid to the clerk. That left one hundred and twenty pounds, eighty-two p. I caught up with the taxi-driver, who charged him eight pounds. He said that Sweetman gave him a two-pound tip, and, unusually, paid him *before* he went in to the bank. That meant that he should have arrived at Cheapos with whatever he had withdrawn from the bank, *plus* a hundred and ten pounds and eighty-two p.'

Angel nodded.

'What did they say at the bank?'

'By the time I got there, it was closed. I phoned them, no reply. Doesn't open until 9.30 in the morning.'

'Catch them first thing.'

'Yes, sir. I had planned to.'

'And what happened at Cheapos?'

'I saw the tape from the CCTV cameras at Cheapos. Sweetman was in shot from the moment he got out of the taxi. He went straight to the booze aisle, took a bottle off the shelf and unscrewed the cap. The chap on security spotted him, and he and another man went down to him. They took him straight to the security room.'

'Did he talk to anybody, a member of staff, a customer . . . anybody?'

'No, sir. He was nowhere near anybody. Nobody could have taken money off him, nor could he have passed anything on to anybody.

He was searched and they couldn't find as much as a two-p piece on him. All this is recorded on tape . . . as clear as day.'

Angel frowned.

'I don't understand it. You know, Ron, it's not *that* long since we could have arrested a man for being a vagrant simply because he hadn't any money on him. That law is probably still on the statute book. I shall want to know exactly what happened to him in the bank ASAP. See to it tomorrow.'

'I'll see to it, sir.'

'Now what about Sweetman's movements during the last fortnight? How far have you got with that? I particularly want to know where he was at the time of the other two fires.'

'I haven't had the chance to get to that, sir.'

'Well, do it *now*,' Angel said impatiently. 'It's going to be a helluva day tomorrow.'

Gawber nodded. He knew that it would be. He stood up.

'Right, sir,' he said and made for the door.

Angel watched the sergeant leave and the door close. He leaned back in the swivel-chair and looked up at the ring of dust on the ceiling around the rose from where the centre light-flex was connected. He rubbed his chin thoughtfully, then he leaned forward in the chair, down it came and he leaned out to pick up the phone. He dialled a number. It was soon answered.

'Fire Service. Can I help you?'

'This is DI Angel, Bromersley police. Can I speak to Chief Fire-Officer Metcalfe?'

'Hold on, sir.'

There was a pause, a short blast of Vivaldi and then a smarmy voice said, 'Metcalfe. Good afternoon, Inspector, now what can I do for you?'

'Ah yes,' Angel said, as pleasantly sincere as he could manage.

Insincerity was very difficult for Angel; he could usually recognize it when he was the recipient, but he couldn't muster the motivation to ladle it out on others. Whereas deceit, he could dispense to crooks, liars and bullies with the greatest of ease without even a twinge of conscience. After all, it was their stock-in-trade; and he was simply using *their* tools against *them*.

'I am just phoning to remind you about the threat to Martin Pennyfeather's home, Chief,' he began. 'As you know, we have had another incendiary-bomb threat. Of course, it may not happen. But the arsonist has delivered on his threat with serious consequences on the last two occasions.'

'Yes indeed,' Metcalfe said.

His ready agreement pleased Angel so he

continued hopefully.

'I expect the assault at 16.30 hours, tomorrow. I wonder, do you think you could have the appropriate appliances and men at Pennyfeather's, say at 16.00 hours . . . so that your men can familiarize themselves with the layout of the house and the sources of water and so on?'

'We have plans on computer of all the water hydrants and natural water resources available to us for the entire district, Inspector. It'll take our station officer only seconds to find them and connect them.'

Angel noticed that this was not going to be as easy as he had first thought.

'Yes, but . . . wouldn't it be safer, quicker and more effective to be there on the spot at the time the incendiary explodes?'

'It certainly would, if there was the certainty of a fire, and the time of its ignition was definite. But, you know, Inspector, if we had to deal with a case like this, we would be pulling out all the stops to prevent the arson. And that's what you should be doing. Prevention would be at the forefront of our strategy. It's you that's in possession of the threatening letter. You are the police. You have all the facilities and know-how. That's where all your effort should be directed. Not calling us in as a sort of insurance back up.'

Angel's lips tightened. So that was the way he wanted to play it. He decided to call his bluff.

'Chief Fire Officer Metcalfe, are you prepared to turn out to Pennyfeather's house tomorrow afternoon or not?'

'Certainly. If there is a fire. We can be there in four or five minutes. But I am not prepared to send appliances out in anticipation that some lunatic fire-raiser, whom you should have caught, may or may not indulge his whim, and lob an incendiary into that house at some arbitrary time that might or might not be 16.30 hours tomorrow afternoon. No. I couldn't do that. I would be committing valuable resources to an incident that may not happen, and in doing so, reduce cover of the remainder of my area. That wouldn't be fair on them. You must understand that, Inspector.'

Angel blew out a long sigh. His lips tightened across his teeth.

'And you must understand this, Chief,' he snarled. 'This is a very unusual and difficult case. We are doing everything possible. Indeed I am personally committed to identifying the guilty party, bringing him to court and getting him a custodial sentence. Sadly, I may not be able to achieve it before the deadline tomorrow. But I would point out to you that we are crime-fighters. You are the fire-fighters. You have the training, the skills and the equipment. It is your job and responsibility to prevent Pennyfeather's home from going up in smoke!'

He slammed down the phone.

★　★　★

About 150 years ago, Branksby Hall had been the home of Lord and Lady Branksby, their eight children and a platoon of servants. Over the years the main house had been converted into a college for adult education and the outbuildings transformed into luxury living-accommodation and leased to anyone who wanted to reside in the countryside and could afford the rent.

Fred Butcher lived in one of the lavish conversions, and Angel was hell-bent on seeing if the once famous, retired illusionist could assist him in his enquiries into the death of Imelda Wilde, who lived only half a mile away in one of the cottages.

He drove the two miles out of Bromersley town centre, past 13 Bottom Bank and up the short hill to the great house. He went through the big wrought-iron gates, past the impressive frontage of the main building, through an arch next to it, into a courtyard, which had a dozen or so apple-green-painted doors that had once been stables on one side. At ninety degrees to the stables was a stone-faced one-storey building that had once been the stable manager's offices and tack-and-feed store, and was now a luxuriously appointed unit of living accommodation.

Angel stopped the car in front of the door and took in the small neatly painted plate screwed into the wall above a doorbell button that read: 'F. Butcher'.

He locked the car, pressed the bell-button with the tip of the umbrella and took a step backwards. There was no immediate reply. He was thinking of pressing it again when the door opened and a tall, broad man in his sixties or seventies with an almost bald head opened the door. He was wearing a red quilted dressing-gown over an open-necked shirt, slacks and red slippers. He was holding a copy of *The Stage* and a pair of spectacle halves. He peered down at Angel with a small smile hanging from his lips. Angel immediately recognized him. He was taller than he had expected. His face was a little fatter and there were a few more creases but it was unmistakably the man he had frequently seen performing big-time magic on the television ten or twenty years ago.

'Mr Butcher?'

'Yes,' he said still smiling.

'I'm Inspector Angel,' he said holding up his warrant card. 'Can I have a few words with you, sir?'

Butcher's eyebrows shot up. The smile left him. He was clearly moved. He pulled the door open further and with a wave of the hand indicated to Angel that he should come in.

'I suppose it's about Imelda Wilde?' he said with a sigh. 'I have been expecting somebody to call.'

'Yes, sir,' Angel replied evenly as he stepped into the hall. He spotted a hallstand with a place for brollies on it and slotted the umbrella into it.

Butcher closed the door and led Angel through the hall into a long, gleaming, bright room that seemed to be a study-cum-sitting-cum-dining-room. There were two big windows looking out to uninterrupted long views of green fields with the Pennines in the distance. In between them was a fireplace that had a flame-effect fire. There was a desk to one side, a wall of books, a dining-table and several easy chairs. The highly polished parquet floor had rugs here and there. Everything was shining and clean.

Butcher dropped the paper he was carrying on to the table in the centre, and put his spectacles in the top pocket of his dressing-gown. He indicated a chair by the window and took the one opposite it.

'This seems very pleasant, Mr Butcher. Do you live on your own?'

'Indeed I do. I fall out with nobody,' he said with a big toothy grin. He had eyebrows that projected over the eyes like a hood, which at times made him look sinister and mysterious.

It was comfortably warm so Angel unbuttoned his coat.

'So you are the great Mysto. I remember seeing you on television. The Great Mysto assisted by Imelda.'

Butcher smiled warmly and said nothing.

'I remember seeing you at the Theatre Royal here in Bromersley. That was the last live show there, I think.'

Butcher shook his head and said: 'That was not the only theatre I closed, regrettably, Inspector.'

'You did all sorts of wonderful tricks, Mr Butcher. I remember your famous Caliph and the Slave Girl illusion. That was very impressive. Where you put Imelda in a box on the stage and in seconds she disappeared from the box and reappeared among the audience.'

'Yes, yes, Inspector,' said Butcher smiling

and appearing to enjoy the nostalgia. 'That was a very difficult illusion, Inspector. And a long time ago.'

'I have always been fascinated by magic and illusions.'

Butcher smiled. 'I've been retired fifteen years now.'

'And never married?'

'Never found the right woman.'

Angel nodded.

'When was the last time you saw Imelda Wilde?'

'It would be last Friday. She brought me some shopping from the supermarket. She put it away for me. I paid her. We had a quick cup of coffee. It was all very . . . very pleasant,' he said sadly.

'Did she seem her usual self?'

'Oh yes.'

'Well, what was your exact relationship with her?'

Butcher smiled.

'She was a very beautiful woman, Inspector, both outside and in. Our partnership . . . our professional partnership goes back a long way. There was never anything romantic between us . . . I mean she was much younger than I was. Let's see, she'd be about forty-eight, now. There was twenty-two years in between us. And look at her. The most beautiful creature you could ever wish to know. She wasn't interested in a lumbering old duffer like me. We were just very good friends.'

Angel nodded.

'What can you tell me about her? How did you meet?'

'Well, I started as Mysto the magician back in the early sixties. And I needed an assistant. A glamorous girl was the obvious ideal contrast to the slightly eccentric and mysterious wizard figure I tried to present to the audiences. Well, I had all sorts of girl assistants . . . mostly star-struck lasses, without a brain in their heads, who thought assisting me would put them in a shop-window for pulling men. And they were right, to a point. But you would have thought I was running a dating-and-mating agency. Some of them had men coming and going in shifts. Men appearing under the beds and out of wardrobes. I told one young man . . . I had to tell him that *I* was the magician. That I had the magic. And I'd make him disappear out of my assistant's room smartly, which I did. Of course, those girls never lasted the course much more than a couple of months. I kept telling my agent to find me a beautiful girl with brains, whom I could completely rely on!'

'You only had the one assistant?'

'Only one at a time, Inspector. If a trick required more than the two of us, I would try to adapt it, or I simply wouldn't do it. It looks impressive to have a team of assistants, but there was always the risk that they might sell the secret of the trick, or break away and start up themselves, and I would find it being performed elsewhere. No, I only ever wanted to have the one assistant. In an ideal world, I would have stayed as I began, on my own. But I wasn't satisfied simply to produce silk handkerchiefs, doves and lighted candles for the rest of my working life. I wanted to move on and up.'

Angel nodded knowingly.

'You said you had an agent?'

'Max Starr. His office is in Leeds. He's still there, I believe. But you wanted to know how Imelda and I met?'

'Yes.'

'Well, I had a summer season at Great Yarmouth. It was 1975. Thirteen weeks, fantastic! I had another new girl called Gwyneth. Very beautiful young thing. We had rehearsed and rehearsed and I had a superb show. The highlight was the elephant illusion. You should have seen it. Maybe you did? I did it on television once, I remember. It was absolutely marvellous, although I shouldn't say it. I made a ten-year-old fully grown African elephant disappear. The audiences were utterly charmed with it and it was easy-peasy. Anyway, I was into the third week and Gwyneth ran off. Left me. In the middle of the season! An old boyfriend from Aberystwyth had turned up. He wanted her to marry him and go and work with him in his father's pie-factory in Swansea or something. Gwyneth's unheralded departure made me into a nervous wreck. I couldn't do the show on my own. Any new girl would have to be carefully rehearsed. Also, at the same time as the summer show, I'd had a contract with Edgar Fromin to appear in one of his Sunday night spectaculars, a twelve-minute spot, *live*! It was big money, Inspector, as well as great exposure. It was that one single show that got me an appearance on the Jay Williams show in America and the subsequent eight-month tour of the US east coast in 1976/77. Anyway, I phoned Max Starr and told him to find me a replacement double quick, and he sent me this beautiful girl dancer from Pudsey. Imelda. Not only was she beautiful, she had style, intelligence and learned so quickly. I couldn't believe my good fortune. The relationship . . . purely a working relationship . . . was excellent. We hit it off straight away.

She was reliable. She put everything she'd got into the show, and I thought the world of her. She even came up with ideas to improve the act. None of the other girl assistants had ever done that.'

'Did she have any family or friends?'

'Her parents, who lived in Pudsey, died about 1990 within a year or two of each other. Imelda told me about it. She was an only one. No brothers or sisters. Friends? Endless men-friends. Especially when we were doing the big venues in London. Every night there would be flowers coming backstage for her, with cards inviting her out.'

'And did she go out with any of them?'

'Oh yes. Lots of them. But she never let her relationships affect her work.'

'Do you know who any of them were? Any special ones? Any you remember by name?'

'She didn't confide that much to me. She knew that I was always concerned that if she married she might leave the act, which was true. There was a lord at one time, I remember. She was in a daze about him . . . until she found out he was married and had four sons . . . all at Eton.'

Butcher laughed gently at the thought of it and then continued:

'Then there was a young man, in the business. She met him when we were working in Manchester. We were doing a week at the Pavilion Theatre. It's closed down now, like everywhere else. Handsome young lad, he was. With his brothers he had a trapeze act. The Consolinos, or something similar. Italian family. They had a very steamy affair, I believe. They used to meet on Sundays. At some hotel half-way between wherever we were booked and they were playing. Eventually it ran out of steam because they had bookings that took him abroad . . . Paris and Berlin and far-flung places. Meeting up regularly became impossible.'

'When was all this?'

'Oh? Twenty years ago, I suppose.'

'Does she have any current boyfriends?'

'I don't know. Bound to have, I would think. But she wouldn't necessarily tell me.'

'What has your relationship with her been lately, then?'

'Well, I had moved here in 1981, when I was doing really well, and at the same time, I organized a cottage down the road for Imelda. It's the same landlord, the Branksby estate. It was convenient then for us to travel together, being four miles from the M1, and six miles from the M62. As the time came round for me to retire . . . it wasn't exactly planned . . . she knew bookings weren't coming in that plentifully any more. Most of the provincial theatres had closed, tenting shows had been greatly reduced because of new laws banning animal acts, television had got fed up with speciality acts . . . magic, jugglers, mind-readers, high-wire artists, acrobats, puppets, ventriloquists, that sort of thing. My retirement was somewhat accelerated by the fact that I was whisked into hospital at short notice to have some troublesome gallstones taken out. I needed a few weeks to recover completely, so I was obliged to get Max to cancel the few bookings he had for us, and, well, that was it. Imelda visited me in hospital and helped me to get re-established back here. Then, since that time, she has done a bit of cleaning and shopping for me. Came up two mornings a week to keep me clean and organized, and . . . well, I shall miss her. I paid her, of course. Yes, I shall miss her. I shall miss her companionship and help very much . . . very much indeed . . . '

'How did she make a living when she was no longer working for you?'

'She had earned a fortune in the good times . . . I expect she put some of it away. She had had a few commissions for modelling . . . more mature stuff. You know, posing next to a successful executive in a suit in building society ad, that sort of thing. I think that work must have dried up; she hadn't talked about it for ages. I paid her a few quid for looking after me, but that wouldn't go far. Thinking about it, she might have been a bit hard-pressed. If she had asked me, I would have helped her out.'

'Have you any idea of any enemies she might have had?'

'No. No enemies. Not Imelda. If she had any enemies at all, they would be men whom she had turned down. Over the years, I suppose she turned down lots of offers.'

9

It was three o'clock when Angel came out of Fred Butcher's. He checked his watch and decided that he still had time to call on Max Starr in Leeds if he got a move on. He was only twenty-four miles away; it wouldn't take long on the M1.

At 3.40 p.m. he was scouring the side streets off The Headrow and eventually spotted an empty parking-space. Delighted, he drove on to it, parked up, locked the car door, pressed the requisite coins in the meter, and strode quickly out towards Fenton Street, using the umbrella as a walking-stick. Two minutes later he turned into the street, past a tobacconists and an office-stationery shop to a once elegant, smoke-stained stone office block called Bramah Buildings. He went through the open wooden doors into the entrance hall where he saw a long wooden sign screwed to the wall. It listed the forty-two tenants who had offices in the block. He found the name *Max Starr and Son, entertainment agents*, discovered that they were on the second floor, went into the old lift and pressed the button. He was soon

161

at the appropriate door with a glass panel with the name he wanted painted in big letters across the glass. He pressed down the door-handle and entered a tiny office.

A young woman with a big bosom, mostly uncovered, was sitting at a desk banging noisily at something. A tin ashtray next to her with a cigarette burning in it was sending up a line of smoke to the brown-stained ceiling. There was a telephone at her elbow. There were two uncomfortable-looking folding chairs, a window looking out at a solicitor's office window across the street, and another door with a glass panel with the word *Private* painted on the glass. The wall space was devoted to framed photographs with names underneath of entertainers of every sort. By the style of the poses and the quality of the sepia, Angel guessed that some of the photographs were more than a hundred years old. A cane waste-paper basket in the corner, and eight square yards of dark red linoleum on the floor completed the room's inventory.

The young woman ignored his entrance. She was engrossed in printing the word *complimentary* across some tickets with a rubber stamp.

Angel was in a hurry. He went up to her desk and said briskly: 'Good afternoon. I want to see Mr Starr. My name is Inspector Angel.'

She stopped the banging and looked up at him with a bored expression.

'Are you an entertainer or a booker?' she whined.

'I'm a *police officer*,' he said pointedly. 'Inspector Angel.'

She gave him an unpleasant look.

'All right. All right,' she said and sulkily reached out for the phone.

He could hear a bell ring out in the adjoining room . . . and he could hear what was said.

'What is it, Maureen?'

'Max, there's a man here says he's from the police. Wants to see you.'

'From the police?'

'That's what he says.'

'Send him in, Maureen.'

Angel didn't wait. He turned round and pressed the door-handle to the inner office.

She replaced the phone.

'He says . . . ' Maureen's raucous voice died away.

A skinny man, with receding hair, aged about fifty, coatless and with his shirt-sleeves rolled up was standing over a big desk, holding a small cigar. He looked across at him and smiled as he came through the door.

'I'm Max Starr. What can I do for you?'

Angel closed the door, came up to the man and flashed his warrant card. 'Inspector Angel, Bromersley Police.'

Starr nodded and pointed to the semicircle of four round-backed upholstered chairs opposite his desk.

'Please take a seat. It'll be about Imelda Wilde,' he said as he sat down in the big swivel-chair. He wrinkled his nose, shook his head, stuffed the cigar back in his mouth and stared across the desk at him.

'Saw it in the paper. Horrible business.'

Angel glanced round the smart little oak-panelled office. It was dominated by the highly polished partner's desk in front of him, on which there were two neat piles of correspondence, a brass desklight, an ashtray and three phones. Flickering in the far corner of the room was a computer screen showing the calendar month of April and the names of major UK towns and cities. In the other corner was an old-fashioned hat-stand with a coat and an umbrella hanging from it. There were six filing-cabinets down the long side of the room next to a stationery cupboard. The old varnished floorboards were part covered with a very well-worn Persian carpet.

'Yes. You were Imelda Wilde's agent?'

'Yes.'

164

'What can you tell me about her?'

He sighed.

'It was a long time since, but I still remember her as if it was yesterday. She came to us here in the mid seventies. She was really an eye-knocker then. My father put her on the books. She was keen to do anything. She'd been trained as a dancer, but she said she'd try anything. He sent her for a try-out with the Great Mysto, Fred Butcher, who was also on our books. He liked her, so my father signed her up. She was on our books until she retired a few years ago. That would be about 1991, when she said she didn't want to work in the business any more.'

'You've not been in touch since?'

'No. Well, we've more than two thousand artists on our books, Inspector. That keeps us pretty busy.'

'And you've not spoken to Fred Butcher about her death?'

'No.'

'What else can you tell me about her?'

'Imelda.' He considered the name thoughtfully. 'Well, she was beautiful, accomplished, lucky, avaricious . . . '

'Avaricious?'

Starr looked awkward, as if he wished he hadn't said it.

'Yes. Always looking for the main chance.

She'd break a date with anybody if say, someone titled or obviously richer came on the scene.'

'She was . . . a gold-digger?'

Starr nodded. 'But I've known worse.'

Angel gave this comment due consideration; Starr was the first to say anything critical of Imelda Wilde.

'Did you know any of her friends?'

'No.'

Angel frowned.

'Did you know any of her relations? Anything about her private life?'

'Only what was on her card. She wasn't married. She lived with her parents in Pudsey before she moved to Bromersley.'

'Have you any idea of anybody who would have wanted her dead?'

'Certainly not.'

Angel rubbed his chin.

'Tell me . . . what sort of a relationship existed between her and Fred Butcher?'

Starr pulled the cigar out of his mouth and smiled.

'Well, I don't think they've ever shared a bed together, if that's what you're getting at.'

'I wasn't getting at anything.'

'There was about twenty years between them. She saw him as a good meal-ticket, that's all. He saw her as a lass who would put money in his wallet . . . which she did. Thousands of pounds. Fred Butcher's not interested in women. He thinks sex is what comes between five and seven. Look at all the girls who've been in his employ. All of them beautiful. They had to be. That was the prerequisite. I never heard one girl say he was the slightest bit interested in them. All Fred wanted to know was that they would be considered glamorous by an audience, would turn up on time and could squeeze into one of his magic cabinets on cue.'

'How did she and Butcher get together?'

'Well, we were his agent from when he started as a beginner in the sixties, producing doves and candles in pubs, working men's clubs and church halls through to the extravaganzas he did for Edgar Fromin on the telly,' Starr replied with a satisfied smile. 'He looked to us to supply glamorous girls to assist him. But he was such a fusspot . . . and he only paid them peanuts. They wouldn't stick it. I swear he was on the phone to us every week for a replacement girl. He got the cream of the crop. But he still wasn't satisfied. Not until Imelda turned up. Dad told him about her, Butcher agreed to give her a try. Dad sent her to the costumier's to get kitted out, then advanced her train-fare to Great Yarmouth and it all started like that.

Fred Butcher took to her like an amateur to applause, and the rest, as they say, is history.'

A thought struck Angel.

'How many girls did he employ?'

'One, in the beginning, then usually two,' Starr said relighting the dead cigar.

'I meant over the years, altogether?'

Starr shrugged. 'The list is a mile long. Well, before Imelda got the job, thirty or forty . . . could be more.'

Angel's eyebrows shot up. 'Forty?' he said.

'Could be fifty. Madame Rita was always making and re-fitting for him, I can tell you.'

'Who is Madame Rita?'

'That's the old crow up Harehills Road. She does costumier work. She made all his girls' flimsy bits they used to wear.'

Angel made a decision.

'I shall want to know all the girls' names.'

'I can do that.'

'And the dates.'

Starr frowned.

'That's a big job, Inspector. But it's no problem. I'll get Maureen to look back through the date-books.'

★ ★ ★

Angel arrived back at the office at twenty past five. He spent a few minutes thinking about

168

the arrangements for the following day and checked off that all the necessary preparations were in hand. There was one item he needed Ahmed to attend to. He would call in the CID office on his way out.

Then he foraged through the large pile of papers on his desk and picked out a yellow booklet produced by the Police Alliance which had arrived by post that morning, entitled: *Proposal for the Amalgamation of the 43 Forces 2006*. He stood up, crossed to his raincoat that was hanging on a hook on the end of the stationery cupboard and stuffed the booklet into the pocket. It would make a spot of reading if there was nothing interesting on the box.

He squared up the rest of the papers on his desk, put them in the drawer and closed it. He had just reached out for his raincoat when he heard a knock at the door. He frowned, turned and called, 'Come in.'

It was Ahmed carrying a sheet of paper.

'I was just coming through to see you, lad, on my way out. I'm going home. What do you want? What's that?'

'MO's report on his examination of the prisoner, Conrad Sweetman, sir,' Ahmed said, holding out the paper. 'Thought you'd want it as soon as it came in.'

Angel licked his lips. He really didn't want

to be bothered with it at that time.

'Yes, ta. Put it on top of that pile in the middle drawer there,' he said pushing an arm through a sleeve in his coat.

Ahmed dutifully obliged.

'You wanted me for something, sir?'

'Yes,' Angel said as he fastened the coat buttons. 'I want everybody involved with tomorrow's operation to have photographs of Lee Wong and Conrad Sweetman. You can copy them from the NPC, can't you?'

'Yes, sir,' Ahmed said, looking soulful. He didn't want to work late that night.

'Well, see to it first thing, lad. It's time you were off now. Get some rest. Big day tomorrow. Don't want you coming in half-baked.'

Ahmed smiled with relief.

'Right, sir. That's about twenty-four of each?'

Angel nodded.

'Good night, lad.'

'Good night, sir.'

The door closed.

Angel sighed, turned to the radiator pipe and lifted Sweetman's umbrella from behind it. He gripped the handle firmly and placed it in position with the tip of it an inch from his shoe. Then he looked down at it. He liked what he saw. He thought the umbrella gave him an air of superiority. He glanced round the room, pursed his lips, nodded, and feeling quite the man about town, stepped smartly out of the office and closed the door.

★ ★ ★

It was 8.28 a.m.

Angel was already in his office finishing off his notes. Thursday 13 April promised to be a big day. He was feeling distinctly uneasy. He sighed. This was the day he hoped to identify and lock up the arsonist . . . whoever it was.

He went through his list again. He rubbed his chin. He seemed to have covered everything. He looked at his watch. He was in good time.

He reached out for the phone and tapped in Ahmed's number. It was promptly answered.

'Good morning, sir. I've finished the prints of Sweetman and Wong . . . they are just drying. Do you want them in there?'

'No, Ahmed. Take them with you to the briefing-room. Now listen up, lad. There's something else. There's something special I want you to do for me.'

'Yes, sir,' Ahmed replied eagerly. He liked the idea of being asked to do something special for Angel. It made him feel important.

'I want you to sit in on the briefing in . . . six minutes' time, so that you know what's happening, and, of course, to distribute the photographs. After that, we shall be setting up an observation and guard at Pennyfeather's house, but I want *you* to stay here. You'll be more valuable to me here than at Pennyfeather's. I want you to monitor Sweetman's movements. He should be taken to court at about ten minutes to ten. Be there. I don't know what time he'll be heard, but I expect it will be before lunch. I expect the magistrates to fine him and release him.'

'Do you want me to follow him, sir?'

Angel smiled. Keen as he was, he didn't think Ahmed would have the skill to follow a wily character like Conrad Sweetman. 'No, lad. No. Just phone me on my mobile and tell me the time he's released from the courthouse. That's all. All right?'

'Yes, sir.'

'And, of course, make yourself available on your mobile all day.'

'Right, sir.'

'Now find DS Crisp and tell him to come into my office, pronto.'

He replaced the phone, opened the desk-drawer and pulled out the pile of papers. On the top was the doctor's report on

Conrad Sweetman. He had forgotten all about it. These doctor's cell reports were usually pretty predictable. He glanced down it quickly. A lot of it was jargon, a lot irrelevant, everything ticked off as normal: the man seemed to be in excellent health. That was OK then. He was about to shove it in the case file when a little handwritten item in blue ink caught his eye. It was an entry in the box headed **Blood Test Result** at the bottom of the page. It was in the doctor's own hand. It read: 'Alcohol content, zero per cent. Other signs confirm. Bloodstream would appear to indicate negative alcohol intake for at least forty-eight hours.'

He read the last sentence again. He couldn't believe it. He read it a third time. Then he rubbed his chin very slowly and very hard. He understood from everybody who had been in contact with Sweetman that the man had been behaving like a professional drunk both here and during the time he had been in a cell at Skiptonthorpe. Everybody had remarked on his noisy, drunken behaviour, his singing and the ever present smell of brandy.

There was a knock at the door. It opened and Crisp's tanned, smiling face showed round the door-jamb.

'You wanted me, sir?'

Angel's face was screwed up with confusion. 'Aye. Come in,' he muttered, frowning.

Crisp's smile left him. He closed the door.

'Read that,' Angel said, pointing at the relevant place on the MO's report.

Crisp took hold of the A4 sheet, looked at the indicated entry, then turned the paper over to see to whom it referred.

'Sweetman?' he queried. 'Hmm. Is this the noisy gent in cell one?'

Angel nodded.

'It says he hasn't had a drink for forty-eight hours at least,' Crisp said with his eyebrows raised. 'That's two days. Could the doc have got it wrong, sir?'

Angel shook his head. 'Shouldn't think so. He's been doing it for thirty years. Ninety per cent of his examination work here is to do with drink or drugs. He knows that's what we call him in for. However, it's usually to tell us how stoned they are, not how sober. I don't understand it.'

'That means the bloke has been acting . . . faking. He's been blurting out 'Nellie Dean' and 'A Scottish soldier', pretending to be drunk for two days to my knowledge.'

'Sweetman's made a fool out of us,' Angel said slowly.

'I'll give him full marks for dedication.'

'Yes, but why?'

Crisp shook his head. 'When you pass his cell it wreaks of . . . er . . . '

'Brandy.'

'Brandy? Nothing but the best. He must have poured it on himself. What a waste.'

'Why?' Angel roared. '*Why?*'

The phone rang. He reached out for it.

'Angel.'

It was the superintendent.

Angel wasn't ready for *him* . . . not this early in the morning and on this particular day.

'Well, lad, are you ready for this . . . fiasco?' Harker said provokingly. 'Everybody's there except you.'

Angel bit his lip. He had to be respectful. And he didn't want to annoy Harker. He couldn't afford to rattle his cage this day of all days. He might need to enlist his support if it all went banana-shaped. 'Gawber's making some last-minute enquiries, so he'll not be there. Crisp's with me. We're coming down now.' He paused a second. 'Are you coming along to Pennyfeather's, sir?'

'Oh no, lad. No. I've better ways of spending my time. It's *your* show. I'll sit in on the briefing, but thereafter, it's up to you.'

There was a click and the phone went dead.

Angel's jaw tightened briefly then he put

175

down the receiver. Nothing new there; as usual, he could expect minimal support from the superinendent. He looked at his watch then turned to Crisp.

'Right, lad. Let's get this show on the road.'

Crisp opened the door, Angel collected the umbrella from behind the pipe and together they went out of the office and down the green corridor to the CID briefing-room.

PC John Weightman was standing in the corridor outside the open door. Angel nodded to him.

'Morning, John. Is the super inside?'

Weightman smiled and said, 'He's right behind you, sir.'

'I'm here, lad,' Harker said, looming up over his left shoulder. Angel noticed a sudden whiff of TCP. It was certain to be coming from him.

He stepped sideways to let him through.

Harker acknowledged the courtesy with a nod and stepped into the noisy room. Angel and Crisp followed him into the sea of black serge and silver buttons. Weightman brought up the rear and closed the door.

Ahmed was standing near the door chatting to PC Scrivens. WPC Leisha Baverstock was at the back, surrounded by laughing male police officers. There was a shushing noise round the room, and the chattering and shuffling stopped as everybody found a chair or positioned themselves conveniently to see and hear the briefing.

Angel raised his eyebrows and looked at Harker, who nodded to him to carry on.

Gripping the umbrella in the middle, Angel looked round the room and began loudly: 'First of all . . . '

There was immediate silence.

He broke off and looked at Ahmed. 'Is everybody here, lad?'

'Twenty-five including the super and you, sir,' Ahmed replied quietly.

That seemed correct. He nodded.

'First of all,' he began, waving the umbrella for emphasis, 'thank you for being so prompt. And some of you, I understand, are coming off your regular duties to assist plain-clothes.'

There was a sarcastic muttering, which was not loud enough for him to hear accurately what was said. It was followed by titters. However, Angel recognized the enjoyment, on the part of the uniformed members, of the puerile jibe that they had had to help plain-clothes out again. He ignored it and pressed on.

'Today, you'll be working under DS Crisp and me. DS Gawber is on some other duty but will be joining us later.'

'In the last two weeks, as you will know,

177

there have been two serious fires, which have gutted the homes of two MPs in the area, and an innocent young woman was seriously burned in one of the fires. She is in the burns unit at the general hospital and is still dangerously ill. Both houses were shelled or assaulted with incendiary bombs type BZ2. The assault occurred after receipt by the householder of a threatening letter, making certain demands that could not be met. Now a third such letter has been received by Mr Martin Pennyfeather, MP for Bromersley, our MP, and a threat has been made on his house — mansion should I say? — out on Elsworth Road, and we have reason to believe that the attack will be made there at 16.30 hours today, although the actual deadline given by the arsonist is ten o'clock this morning. So we need to be on our toes thereafter.

'Our job is to search Martin Pennyfeather's house, outbuildings and grounds, which are extensive, before the expiry of the deadline, then seal them off, so that there is no chance of the arsonist being already hidden on the premises or subsequently gaining access. I must warn you that this man is dangerous. If he succeeds a third time, there is no saying what deaths or injuries may occur or what damage may be inflicted. The fire-service have been notified and will attend promptly in the event of a fire.

'The arsonist may arrive disguised, even in police uniform, therefore I urge you to get to know each other and not to accept the presence of an unknown face without question. We have two major suspects, and PC Ahmed Ahaz has photographs of both of them. There are copies for everyone. Please collect one of each on your way out. They are Lee Wong, who was a political agitator and general nuisance, who has served time for disturbance of the peace and similar charges, and Conrad Sweetman, who has served time for fraud and D and D and, coincidentally, will be in our local magistrates court again this morning, where I expect he will be fined again and then released from custody. Don't underestimate either of them. In addition to the team here assembled, we have the assistance of two patrol cars. They will be on call and will be patrolling the perimeter walls of Mr Pennyfeather's estate from 09.50 hours. PC John Weightman will be on the gate. He'll be in touch directly with me on my mobile. That will be the only means in and out of the house and grounds after 09.50 hours.

'DC Crisp will accompany you and, on arrival, will supervise the searching of the outbuildings, garden and copse, and arrange the posting. At postings of two hundred yards to the next man, we shall have absolute visible coverage of the entire perimeter of the estate. You only have to watch out for any intruder or stranger, and arrest them.

'DC Gawber, on his arrival will search the house with two constables. I expect to be in the house near the target position. I think that's about it. Now are there any questions?'

A voice called out from the back.

'Yes, sir. What exactly does the bomb look like, sir?'

Angel nodded. 'Yes. Good question. The bombs used in the previous fire-attacks were sixteen inches long, four and a half inches wide, and weighed six pounds ten and a half ounces. An interesting thing about those bombs: whereas bombs are usually a natural grey metal colour and sprayed with light oil or wrapped in a grease-coated paper, these bombs had been cleaned off and sprayed with white paint.'

There were mutters of surprise and interest.

'Now are there any other questions?'

He looked round. Apparently not.

'Right, thank you. There are three personnel-carriers at the front of the station to take you the two-mile journey. Please go straight there, there is no time to lose.'

10

Angel pressed the bell-button with the tip of the umbrella from which he was reluctant to be separated even though there was no sign of rain. The bell was not immediately answered, so he stood back and looked round behind him. At his elbows were three uniformed PCs eager to get on with searching the house and sealing it off. Behind them, more police were piling out of the personnel-carriers and stomping noisily on the gravel. DC Crisp was marshalling them to start the search of the outbuildings and grounds.

Eventually the house door opened and Angel turned back to see a lady of mature years in an overall standing there wiping her hands on a tea-towel. When she saw Angel, the three officers and the army behind, her mouth dropped open.

'Can I see Mr Pennyfeather, please? He is expecting me. I'm Inspector Angel, Bromersley police.'

She quickly recovered.

'Oh yes,' she said politely. 'He said to expect you, please come in. I'm Mrs Hargreaves, Mr Pennyfeather's housekeeper.

You want to search the house again, don't you?'

'Pleased to meet you, Mrs Hargreaves. Yes, that's right. But I would like to see Mr Pennyfeather first, if that's possible.'

'He isn't here, I'm afraid. Joined his family at his wife's sister's in Rotherham, you know.'

Angel frowned. He was very surprised.

'Really?'

He had expected the man to be there on hand to help him and his men try to catch the monster who would attempt to burn down his house and home . . . even if it was only by giving moral support. He shook his head, then ran the tip of his tongue along his bottom lip. Was there something inherently shifty about wealthy MPs . . . ? Or was it just Martin Pennyfeather? Perhaps it was simply that he and his wife and their two children could so easily bunk up with his wife's sister, Elinor Goosen. She was the flashy, rich bitch frequently showing off her cleavage on the covers of *Money Investment Monthly* and *Glass and Plastic Mouldings*, and who, with her father and her sister Primrose, owned most of the shares in Goosen's Glass plc. Angel supposed that they were so well heeled that if Mr Pennyfeather's house went up in smoke, the Pennyfeathers needn't worry a jot. Mr P would simply claim for all new sticks and stones on the insurance. And that would be that. For that fortunate family, a crisis like this just seemed far too easy.

'He isn't here?' Angel repeated abstractedly.

'My husband's downstairs in the kitchen. He'll do anything you may want him to do. He's very handy. Does the garden and grounds for Mr Pennyfeather, you know.'

Angel smiled. That was indeed a very kind offer.

'Thank you, Mrs Hargreaves. There's nothing I can think of, at the moment.' He turned to the three men. 'Right, lads, carry on. Start at the top floor and work down. Every cupboard, wardrobe, every nook and every cranny. Anywhere where a person could hide. Close and lock all windows. Close and lock all doors. As you search a floor, one of you guard the landing so that nobody can pass you.'

They dashed off up the stairs, eager to get started.

He turned back to the housekeeper.

'Is there anybody else in the house, apart from your husband?'

'Oh no. They've been given the day off.'

'Right,' said Angel. 'I will want you and your husband to join us in the drawing-room at 09.50 hours and be prepared to stay there

183

throughout the day.'

'I don't know about all day, Inspector,' she said, shaking her head. 'I've got my work to do.'

'For your own safety,' he added sternly. He crossed to the drawing-room door and opened it. 'Is there a phone in there?'

'Not at the moment, but I can take one from another room and plug it in for you.'

'Please do that, Mrs Hargreaves. We have our own mobiles, but it would be good to have back-up.'

'Hmm. There's only twenty minutes. I'll nip off and make some sandwiches and tea.'

Angel smiled and nodded.

'That would be nice.'

'I'll get my husband to bring it up,' she said and rushed out.

Angel followed her out into the large imposing entrance hall, thoughtfully swinging the umbrella. He looked first down at the marble floor. The incendiary bombs in the other two houses had been detonated in the hall. The arsonist certainly knew what he was doing. The ideal location to start a fire, if you want to burn a mansion down . . . draped curtains, carpets, wooden banisters, stairs, hall table. Heat rises. Draws all the way up the stairwell. It would spread to all the floors and the building would be an inferno in no time. He never wanted to see it happen, especially on that day.

He made his way through the open door into the big drawing-room and looked over the sea of comfortable chairs. His mobile rang. His eyebrows shot up. He dived into his pocket, pulled it out and flicked open the cover.

'Angel.'

'Ah, yes, lad.'

It was Harker.

Angel's face changed.

'Are you all set then?' said Harker brusquely.

'Almost, sir. Yes,' replied Angel. He wondered why the superintendent had phoned. There would be more to it. It was only twenty minutes since he had seen him at the briefing.

'Good. Good,' Harker replied, then his tone changed. He hesitated. 'Erm . . . I've just had a phone call from the hospital. That young lass, the *au pair* who was injured in that fire at Beston North . . . she's died.'

Angel blew out a foot of breath. That was unexpected. He didn't like that. A young woman in her twenties.

'That's bad,' he said, thoughtfully lowering himself into an easy-chair.

'Worse,' Harker said. 'It now means your

arsonist is also wanted for murder.'

Angel pursed his lips. Yes, of course he was.

'I appreciate you letting me know, sir.'

'Yes.' Harker grunted.

The phone clicked and the superintendent was gone.

Angel sighed again. A girl in her twenties. Awful.

He closed the phone and returned it to his pocket.

He looked round at the big, comfortable room with its many big easy-chairs, settees and small tables. It was unexpectedly quiet. He felt very much alone in the big room. His pulse was drumming insistently in his ears. Something ominous was imminent. He knew it. He would be happy to get that day over.

There was a noise in the hall . . . footsteps approaching. It was Mrs Hargreaves. She came through the open drawing-room door carrying a telephone with a coil of flex.

'I've taken this from the study,' she said. She crossed the room, plugged the flex into a socket in the skirting-board, put the phone on a wine-table, then lifted the table with the phone on it over to where Angel was sitting. 'There you are,' she said. She straightened up and made her way to the door.

He thanked her.

A few seconds later she was gone.

His mobile rang.

'Angel,' he said.

It was the superintendent again.

'Just heard from the clerk of the court. Thought you'd like to know that Sweetman has been fined eighty pounds and given twenty-four hours to pay the fine. The magistrate has given him a severe warning and handed him over to the probation service for supervision.'

Angel rubbed his chin.

'That means he's out.'

'Free as a bird, lad. Free as a bird.'

Angel didn't like that. Didn't like it one bit.

Harker said: 'Have you seen or heard anything of Lee Wong?'

Angel thought about Sweetman being free, and if and when he might expect him to attempt to set fire to the house. Ahmed was supposed to be monitoring him. What was Ahmed up to? He should have phoned.

'Are you there?' Harker bawled. 'I said have you seen anything of Lee Wong?'

'Sorry, sir. No I haven't seen anything of Wong.'

'Mighty funny business, if you ask me.'

Angel agreed.

'Yes, sir.'

'Well, you'd better catch *something* today . . . and I don't just mean a cold.'

The line went dead.

Angel closed his mobile thoughtfully. He was still wondering why Ahmed hadn't phoned.

An electric bell rang persistently from some distant part of the house. At the same time there was the loud banging of a knocker on the front door. He dashed into the hall to investigate. At the same time he heard footsteps running up the basement steps. It was Mrs Hargreaves. He guessed that the bell he had heard ringing was in the basement and was triggered by the bell-push on the front door.

'It's all right, Inspector Angel, I'll get it,' she said, virtually racing him to the door.

He let her win and watched her turn the big key and then the knob.

Gawber and Crisp burst in together. They had apparently met on the step.

'Now, now, what's all that noise about?' she said.

'Thank you, Mrs Hargreaves,' Angel said. 'These two gentleman are with me.'

They smiled their thanks at her.

She nodded, closed the door and made off down the stairs to the basement.

Gawber's face was red and his eyes shone as Angel had never seen them shine before.

'Sir,' he began. He couldn't wait to get

through the door before he started speaking. 'You're not going to believe this. I phoned Skiptonthorpe nick to find out the exact dates and times of Conrad Sweetman's arrest and release from there. I intended to construct a chart to follow his movements, as you had instructed. It turned out that he was there, locked up in a cell at the times of the fires . . . both at Mantelborough on 4 April *and* at Beston North on 10 April.'

Angel stared at him. It was unbelievable!

'I tried to phone you, several times, but you were always engaged,' Gawber added.

Angel looked stunned. He shook his head slightly and said nothing.

Crisp said: 'That means Sweetman's in the clear, sir. It's good news, really. It clarifies the situation. All this time you've been worrying about him and whether he was the arsonist or whether it was Wong, and now you know. He's got the perfect alibi. At the critical times, on both occasions, Sweetman was locked up in a police cell in Skiptonthorpe nick. That's clear enough.'

Angel looked at Crisp but still said nothing. He turned and walked slowly towards the drawing-room door. He found a chair and sat down. He put the umbrella carefully across the top of the coffee-table.

Gawber and Crisp followed him through

and sat down opposite.

'And I checked up at the bank, sir,' Gawber continued. 'The reason why he had no money on him at Cheapos was that after he had paid the taxi he made out a paying-in slip in the bank and paid a hundred and ten pounds, eighty-two p into his own account. It was clearly a deliberate move to leave himself without money.'

Crisp nodded knowingly.

'The old vagrant trick.'

Angel's face tightened.

'Well, it hasn't worked for him,' he said. 'He's not locked up this time. The super's just phoned to say he's been fined, warned, put on probation and released.'

'So,' Crisp said thoughtfully. 'Even though he couldn't have set fire to the other two houses, he is now free to attempt to set fire to *this* house?'

'Yes, but it lacks a certain simple logic, doesn't it?' Gawber said.

'And consistency,' Angel added.

Gawber said: 'Well, sir, it doesn't matter, does it, sir? He was locked up when the other fires were started so he's definitely not our arsonist.' He pointed to the umbrella that Angel had earlier carefully placed on the table between them. 'He might have an umbrella-and-rice fetish,' he said lightly, 'but that

190

would be another story.'

Gawber looked at Crisp who smiled, they both looked at Angel, who didn't.

Angel eased back in the chair and slowly rubbed his chin. There was something strange happening. Everything had pointed to Sweetman being the arsonist, and now up came proof that it couldn't have been. It should have been a relief, but it wasn't. It had just made the muddy waters muddier. It was exasperating. However, you couldn't argue with facts, and he could trust Ron Gawber and the lads at Skiptonthorpe to know what they were talking about. It now meant that once and for all, he could dismiss Sweetman from his mind and concentrate on the other suspect, Lee Wong. He must be caught as soon as possible. He blew out a long breath and turned to Crisp. 'Are all your men in position?'

'Yes, sir. All the outbuildings and grounds searched. Nobody will get in or out of the grounds without being spotted. Nobody goes through that gate without big John Weightman knows all about it. All strangers will be detained until we can OK their identity and business.'

Angel nodded. He was pleased about that. Crisp seemed to know exactly what his role was.

'Right,' Angel said. 'Get back out there, keep them on their toes. I don't want so much as a ladybird sneaking past them over that wall, you understand. You can tell them it's the Chinese-looking man, Lee Wong, to watch out for. Arrest him on sight and be very careful. You never know, he might try to gain entry in disguise. And, by the way, if you think it will help, you can tell them he's wanted for murder as well as arson. The *au pair* died this morning.'

Gawber and Crisp glanced at each other briefly, but said nothing.

Angel's mobile began ringing.

Crisp looked at Angel.

'Carry on, lad,' Angel said as he dived into his pocket again, pulled out the phone, opened it and pressed the button.

Crisp went out into the hall. The front door closed.

It was Ahmed. Angel was not pleased with him.

'You were supposed to phone me,' he barked into the mouthpiece, 'and tell me what happened to Sweetman in court. As it is, the super rang and — '

'I couldn't get through, sir. Sweetman was released at 10.20, sir,' Ahmed burst in excitedly, and he clearly had something more to say.

'I knew that, lad. You're too late — '

'Did you know that he kicked PC Mowler on the shin, sir, because he said he was trying to intimidate him, and he drew blood, so the sergeant rearrested him, put him back in the cell to cool off, and is now charging him with assault?'

Angel couldn't believe what he had heard.

'What?' he bawled.

Gawber stared at him.

Angel shook his head. He took his time to reply. He didn't know what to say. 'Is he in a cell now?'

'Yes, sir. The sergeant says he must be drunk or mental.'

Angel blinked knowingly, but didn't tell Ahmed what he knew. 'All right. Keep me posted.'

'Right, sir. Goodbye.'

Angel closed the mobile and thrust it in his pocket. He thought for a moment then told Gawber what Ahmed had told him.

Gawber was equally astonished.

'There's something very odd about Sweetman, sir,' he said. 'But his alibis are absolutely cast-iron.'

'What if he is still in the nick at 4.30 this afternoon?'

'Makes no difference. He definitely didn't bomb the other two houses. Why would you still expect him to be responsible for an attempt on this one?'

Angel had to nod in agreement. He didn't reply further to the rhetorical question. His thoughtful demeanour was sufficient. He scratched his head. It was odd how you got ideas about people. Hard to shake them off. But now that Sweetman was no longer in the frame, Lee Wong had to be favourite, (didn't the Chinese invent fireworks, anyway?) Indeed, he was the only suspect they had, and he had disappeared from the face of the earth. It would be like Wong to penetrate their defences, set up a mortar, aim it accurately, send up a shell and set fire to the place. He could be in the house now. Concealed in some specially prepared hiding-place. Behind a false panel in the back of a wardrobe. A space under the stairs. Fred Butcher could have advised him about the concealment of a person in a small space. He hadn't thought of it earlier. He couldn't consult him now. There wasn't time. *Time*. How was the enemy? He checked his watch and turned to Gawber.

'The team of three, searching the house, Ron, check up on them. See if they've found anything. They should have finished by now.'

Gawber nodded and rushed off.

194

It was 3.30 p.m., five and a half hours after the arsonist's ultimatum had expired and an hour before the expected time of a bomb attack.

The team of three PCs, having completed the search of Pennyfeather's house and finding no person hidden nor anything at all relevant to a possible attack, had been directed to observing the front garden and beyond from the two bay windows in the drawing-room.

The small gathering was enjoying tea and sandwiches prepared by Mrs Hargreaves. They were being served by her and her husband from a hostess trolley that Mr Hargreaves had wheeled through from the dining-room next door. He had made himself known to Angel and Gawber and seemed to be a willing assistant to his wife, showing a deferential interest in anything and everything that was happening on that unnerving day.

Gawber was in a corner of the room, speaking by mobile phone to the co-driver of one of the two cars that were patrolling the area around the Pennyfeather estate. The news from that car was negative, which was no surprise to him. He terminated the conversation, closed the phone and came over to the inspector.

Angel was drinking tea, running short on patience and wondering what might be done to speed the waiting game and avoid a third incendiary bomb being fired.

'Nothing to report, sir. No sign of anything untoward,' Gawber said monotonously.

Angel made up his mind.

He placed the cup and saucer noisily on the coffee-table in front him. 'Hold the fort, Ron,' Angel said. 'I am going to see Wong.'

★　★　★

He parked the car right outside the Golden Cockerel, reached out for the umbrella, locked the car and ran up the steps and through the doors. The restaurant was busy; more than half the tables had customers seated at them. All the stools at the bar were occupied.

The beautiful Margarita greeted him at the door. She bowed her head and smiled as she did to all visitors.

'I want to see Mr Wong.' Angel said hurriedly.

'One moment, please, Inspector. I will enquire,' she said with her usual overdone obsequious charm. She turned to a passing waiter carrying a tray of covered plates and rattled off something in a high-pitched

196

squeaking voice. The waiter responded in like fashion and rushed away to serve his customers.

Margarita turned back to Angel.

'Where is he?' he asked her impatiently.

'He is in the kitchen with a man from the weighing-scales company, Inspector. I'll have him come to you straight away.'

Angel knew the way to the kitchen.

'Don't bother, miss, I'll find him,' he said. Raising the umbrella in front of him, he cut across the restaurant floor, picking his way between the busy tables. He found the 'in' door to the kitchen and pushed his way through it.

There was a lot of noise inside the kitchen, the sound of shouting voices, the rattle of plates and cutlery, the sizzle of cooking, the running of taps, the hissing of steam. Exotic smells teased the nostrils as a dozen men and girls in spotless white overalls and hats were working quickly at benches or in front of ovens and hotplates. Some turned round, saw Angel, stared at him rudely and some shouted at him in Chinese. They were not pleased to see him. He was not welcome in the kitchen when they were working at high speed.

Angel saw the sharp-suited Harry Wong talking animatedly to a man in blue overalls, who appeared to be an engineer. They were standing in front of a catering weighing-scale with a big dial. A case of engineer's tools was open on the floor and various brass-coloured testing-weights were spread across the work-top and the floor. There appeared to be a controversy of some kind. Wong turned, saw Angel; his face showed that he wasn't pleased to see him.

Angel made his way, passing a cloud of steam from a boiling pan, across the kitchen. He came up close to Wong who moved away from the weighing-scale engineer.

'Where is Lee?' Angel called out, waving the umbrella.

'Inspector, you shouldn't be in here. Nothing has happened yet, has it? There is a problem with our scales. I will see you in my office. It will be private there.'

Angel gave no indication that he intended moving. 'Where is Lee?' he repeated. 'Is he here?'

'No, of course not. Has an attempt been made on the house yet?'

'No. Where is your son?' Angel persisted.

Wong seemed relieved.

'I have no idea. He has not turned up. You should speak with that Conrad Sweetman. *He*'s the man you want.'

'No.'

'When you have Sweetman arrested for arson and Lee sees it reported in the media, I am certain he will return to us.'

Angel shook his head.

'The fires were not started by Sweetman. You've been wasting my time, Harry. At the times those incendiaries were being shelled into those houses, Sweetman was in a cell in Skiptonthorpe, under police supervision, locked up. It could not possibly be him. I think it was your son, Lee. He was the one who has the grudge. He was the one who wrote the letters. And he is the one who has run off in spite of all our appeals to him. And I think you and your wife know all about it and are sheltering him.'

Wong's face went white.

'Not so, Inspector. We have no idea where he is. And it isn't in him to behave in this way. I have told you.'

Angel was brooking no nonsense.

'I have to tell you that your son is not only wanted for arson, he is now also wanted for murder,' he said emphatically. 'The young girl badly burned at the Beston End fire died this morning of her injuries.'

Wong looked down at the floor and shook his head.

'If your son goes ahead with this arson attack on Pennyfeather's house today,' Angel continued angrily, 'I shall do everything in my power to see that he gets put down for twenty years!' He shouted the last words, waving the umbrella at Wong.

Wong stared back at him defiantly.

Suddenly, Angel noticed that the kitchen noises behind him had died down. He looked round. Everybody's eyes were on him. He saw the two heavies, who Wong had previously told him were waiters, coming towards him from the door. The engineer in the blue uniform repairing the weighing-scale came forward wielding a spanner. Some of the cooks had found dangerous-looking spoons, ladles and knives, were holding them tightly and staring at him. The female kitchen-workers were cowering together, holding hands by the cold-room door.

Wong asserted himself and shouted something in Chinese.

Everybody froze.

Angel realized for the first time that he was potentially in great danger. His heart was banging away and his mouth was as dry as the rice in the umbrella.

Wong forced a smile. He turned it into a grin. It was all very false.

'I believe they thought you were going to assault me with that umbrella, Inspector,' he said very quietly. 'I respectfully suggest that you offer it to me. I will take it and put it down, say on the scales behind me, momentarily.'

Angel hesitated. But he decided it was the only possible thing to do. He slowly passed the umbrella to Wong, who waved it in the air triumphantly. Angel watched, concerned in case he spilt out any of the rice. Then Wong put it in the big, shiny, silver bowl of the kitchen scales. The dial moved a little way, much to the irritation of the engineer.

There was a second of quiet and then the kitchen staff turned from one to the other, muttered something; there were a few smiles, they nodded and quickly returned to work.

Angel sighed.

'I must go, Mr Wong.'

The engineer took the umbrella out of the bowl and handed it back to Angel.

The inspector smiled and came through the kitchen door, feeling very relieved and with a light heart.

Realization dawned on him.

It was as if the beautiful girl had leaped out of the exploding cake and twelve high-kicking lamé-dressed young women danced across the restaurant floor towards him.

11

At last, some progress had been made and he was feeling ten years younger. He felt vital and buoyant again. He was flying high. Life was great.

Five minutes later, at 16.10 hours, Angel arrived back at Pennyfeather's. He pulled up outside the main gate.

Big John Weightman recognized the car and went over to the open window.

'Everything all right, sir?'

Angel nodded brightly.

'Anything happening here?'

'No, sir. All quiet on the western front.'

'Well, it's not over yet, John. I am expecting an attack in about twenty minutes. Be particularly watchful then.'

Weightman nodded.

'I will, sir.'

He opened the gate.

Angel drove up to the front door and rang the bell. Mrs Hargreaves let him in. He thanked her and charged straight into the drawing-room.

Gawber came across to him.

'Everything all right here, Ron?'

'Yes, sir. Quiet as a grave. Cup of tea?'

'That would be nice. Yes, please.'

Gawber wandered away to find Mr or Mrs Hargreaves.

Angel quickly put the umbrella down on the table, unfastened his coat, began feeling about in his pockets for his mobile. He came across the photographs of Lee Wong and Conrad Sweetman. He pulled them out and tossed them on the table, he didn't need them any more. He then found his mobile and dialled the superintendent's direct number.

The voice of a chimpanzee with haemorrhoids answered.

'What is it?' Harker muttered. 'What's happened?'

'It'll happen at 16.30 hours, sir.'

'I think you're wasting time, lad.'

Angel wrinkled his nose. He did dislike this man.

'I understand that Conrad Sweetman was released this morning, sir, but as the result of some fracas . . . he kicked an officer, PC Mowler I believe, and was rearrested.'

'Yes. That's right. He's in a cell now. Charged with assaulting a police officer. Why?'

'Well, sir, I have found out that he was in Skiptonthorpe nick on both occasions when the other two fires were started, charged with being drunk and disorderly . . . also, when he was in our nick yesterday, that he wasn't actually drunk . . . '

'Oh, wasn't he? Well, so what, lad. What are you getting at?'

'Well, sir, if he's locked up . . . and it looks as if he *wants* to be locked up, he can't start fires, can he?'

'What is this, twenty bloody questions?'

'No sir, I wondered, if you . . . and the desk sergeant and PC Mowler could agree . . . I wondered if you would drop the charge of assault . . . and release Conrad Sweetman. Let him go free. Immediately. Now.'

'Well, we could, I suppose, but what would be the point of that?'

'Well, if he's free, sir, he wouldn't have an alibi, would he? And that's what he's trying to establish. You see, he must have an accomplice or have some way of launching the incendiary from inside his cell. If he's free, we can pick him up and charge him. But you'd have to let him go now or he wouldn't actually be free at 16.30 to start the fire.'

'If he's locked up, he won't be able to set fire to anything, will he?' Harker replied strongly. 'Besides, it isn't him who is the arsonist, is it? It's the Chinese lad, Lee Wong. That's the chap you've got to look out for.

I've told you that and I keep telling you!'

'Oh no sir. The arsonist is definitely Conrad Sweetman. If you release him now, I can catch him in the act. If you don't . . . '

'I think you're losing your grip, lad. I can't possibly release a man charged with assaulting one of my police officers. And your flimsy tale cuts no ice with me. I know that you're in a hole. I can see that that expensive exercise you have mounted is going to be a complete waste of time and will prove to be very . . . embarrassing, but — '

'That's not it at all. I know now that Conrad Sweetman is the arsonist. I just need to catch him in the act to prove it.'

'If it means letting him off a charge of assault and releasing him so that he can come and set fire to Pennyfeather's place, to test some new cock-eyed theory of yours, then the answer is definitely no. And if you're not ready for the loony bin, Angel, I don't know who is. Now buck yourself up, lad, forget these stupid ideas, put today's operation down to a mistake, dismiss the team and report back here.'

The diatribe finished with a loud click in his ear.

Angel closed the phone and stuffed it in his pocket. He slumped angrily in the chair.

Hargreaves wheeled the trolley across to

where he was sitting, picked up the teapot and began pouring. 'The sergeant said you wanted a fresh cup, Inspector.'

Angel didn't see him. He couldn't respond. His mind was in turmoil.

Hargreaves finished pouring, added milk and then hovered over the table looking for a coaster. He saw the two photographs that Angel had thrown down. He picked one up and stared at it.

'This one of the chaps you're looking for?' he said casually.

Angel noticed him, took the tea and nodded. 'Thank you,' he said automatically.

'I've seen him,' Hargreaves said quietly.

Angel looked up.

'Oh?'

'Yes. A couple of days ago. Works for the gas company. Came here in a big gas board lorry.'

Angel blinked. His heart missed a beat. He banged the cup and saucer down on the table.

'Are you sure it was him?'

'Oh yes,' Hargreaves said.

'He came here? To this house?' Angel said incredulously.

'Yes, sir.'

'You let him *inside*?'

'Yes,' said Hargreaves artlessly.

Angel's pulse began to race.

'Well tell me all about it . . . just a minute.' He stood up, looked across the room and called out, 'Ron, come here, quickly. Bring those three men.'

Gawber was with the PCs watching through the bay windows. They heard the summons and recognizing the urgency in Angel's voice rushed across the room to him with worried looks. Mrs Hargreaves realized something was happening involving her husband, stopped dusting, and joined the group.

'Listen to this, everybody. Sweetman's been here. Inside this house. Please go on, Mr Hargreaves, quickly.'

'He was here . . . in overalls, too big for him. He's not very tall. And he wore a red dicky-bow . . . like in the photograph. And polished shoes. I thought it was unusual for a gasman to have polished shoes.'

'Yes. Yes. And what did he want?'

'It was just after Mrs Pennyfeather had left to take Mr Pennyfeather to Doncaster to catch the train for London. I was in the kitchen with the missis. The front door-bell rang. I answered it. There was this man on the step. Ever so smart he was, and he spoke well. He said there had been a dangerous gas explosion two streets away due to some gas piping that should have been renewed. The gas board didn't want a repeat of the explosion. So for our safety, he was checking all the houses on the same supply, and he needed to check on the gas pipes in the house. It was desperately important, he said. It would take about twenty minutes. There didn't seem to be much choice about it, so I let him in. The boss would want the house safe. And he had proper gas board uniform and a company vehicle. I thought he was the genuine article.'

Angel nodded, looked at Gawber and said, 'That would be the stolen vehicle the super had been on about.' He turned back to Hargreaves. 'Whereabouts did he go in the house?'

'I didn't stay with him. I don't know. I had the lawns to cut. I asked him to ring the bell when he was ready for off. I told the missus, and she thought what I had done was the right thing.'

He looked at her, she nodded in accord.

'Then I went into the tool-shed out back and brought out the lawn-mower and started on the big lawn. I saw him drive off about twenty minutes later. He gave me a wave. I took it from that that everything had been checked and that the house was safe.'

'Far from it,' Angel muttered grimly.

'Thank you very much, Mr Hargreaves. That means, almost certainly, that Sweetman has somehow interfered with the gas and/or electricity supply, planted a bomb or a timed explosive device, or smuggled in an accomplice to effect an explosion! *The devil.*'

Everybody drew in breath.

Mrs Hargreaves said: 'Oh!'

Hargreaves's mouth dropped open.

Angel looked at his watch.

'Ron, we have only eight minutes!'

Gawber's heart began to pound.

Angel turned to Hargreaves.

'Where is the gas-meter and boiler?'

'In the basement.'

'Do you know how to turn them off?'

'I think so, yes.'

'Do it. Do it, now. Be careful. If you see anything unusual on or near the equipment, let me know.'

'Right,' Hargreaves said and dashed off.

He turned to Mrs Hargreaves and the others.

'We need baths, bowls, pans, anything that can be used as a container. They need to be filled with water. They need to be out there in the hall.'

'Why the hall, sir?' one of the PCs asked.

'Don't know. The other bombs always exploded in the hall,' he said quickly. Then he

209

turned to Gawber. 'Check the hall windows are securely locked again.'

'Yes, sir,' Gawber said.

'And sand. We need a lot of sand, builder's ordinary sand, seaside sand, sand, lots of sand. And shovels! And buckets. Go on, chaps. Get cracking. No time to waste. This house could be like hell itself in seven minutes!'

Mrs Hargreaves grasped the initiative.

'Right, lads. Follow me,' she said. 'I'll tell you where everything is.'

The four policemen dashed out of the drawing-room behind her. 'There's some stuff in the summer-house,' he heard her call as their feet clattered across the marble floor in the hall on their way to the basement stairs. 'And there's pans and things out in the kitchen!'

Angel dived into his pocket, pulled out his mobile, tapped in a number and listened out for a reply. He was breathing heavily. Thank God it was answered promptly.

It was a woman's voice.

'Emergency. Fire. Police. Ambulance. Which service do you require?'

'Fire,' he said impatiently.

'Fire? Hold on, caller. Putting you through.'

A man's voice came on the line.

'Fire service. What is the address of the fire, please?'

'This is Detective Inspector Angel of Bromersley Police. There isn't actually a fire yet.'

'What? There isn't a fire?' the man said gruffly.

'No. Not yet.'

'Is this some sort of a lark? Get off the line then. This is for emergencies only. This line must be kept absolutely free. I shall report this to the police.'

'I *am* the police,' stormed Angel.

'If you are, you'd know that this line is exclusively for reporting fires . . . '

'I want to report that a fire is *imminent*. It's at . . . '

'We don't put out fires that are imminent. We put out fires that are real and burning and causing damage to people or their property. Now get off the line. You're blocking callers who may have a *real* fire to report.'

The line went dead.

Angel went scarlet. He snapped the phone shut and stuffed it in his pocket. He sighed. His heart felt as heavy as a cannon ball.

It was 16.27 hours.

'Can you see *anything*, lad? Is there *anybody* at all out there? . . . a stranger of any sort out there? Anything unusual?' Angel

211

blurted into his mobile, while walking up and down the drawing-room.

'No, sir. Nothing unusual,' Crisp replied.

Angel shook his head.

'Very well. There are about three minutes to go. Tell your men, be on their guard. Phone me if you see anything unusual, anything at all. If a sparrow passes wind, *I want to know about it.*'

'Right, sir.'

Gawber came into drawing-room. He was perspiring and red in the face.

Angel closed down the mobile.

'Everything ready?'

'They're just filling an old bath with water, sir. We can't do any more. We've filled three sacks with sand. Mr Hargreaves has found some spades and rakes . . . Mrs Hargreaves has come up with an assortment of pans and bowls which we've filled with water . . . '

Angel said, 'Good. Good. I've spoken to both patrol cars, John Weightman on the gate and Crisp who is on another round and there's absolutely nothing on the move out there.'

Gawber was wiping his forehead with his handkerchief. 'Do you *really* think Sweetman can start a fire while locked up in a cell in our nick, sir?'

Angel wrinkled his nose and sighed.

'Sounds impossible, I know. Possibly a timing device. There must be a way.'

'There wasn't a timer on those other two incendiaries. Are you *certain* it's not Lee Wong?' Gawber said, pursing his lips.

Angel turned the corners of his mouth down. 'Absolutely positive. I don't know *how* he does it, but it's Sweetman for certain.'

Gawber frowned.

'You'd better call your men and Mr and Mrs Hargreaves in here. We all need to take cover now. Did you check on those windows out in the hall?'

'Yes, sir. They're both closed and locked,' he said as he went out of the drawing-room.

Angel tapped a number into his mobile.

Ahmed's concerned voice answered quickly. 'Are you all right, sir?'

The young constable's concern comforted and pleased him.

'Of course,' he said, grandly. He didn't want to show any sign of anxiety to the young man. 'So far, so good. It's almost time. Ahmed, I want you to go quickly down to the cells and look at the man in cell two. Take your phone with you. I'll hold on.'

'Right sir. I am on my way.'

Gawber came back into the drawing-room with the two PCs and Mr and Mrs Hargreaves and closed the door. They looked at Angel who, with a gesture, suggested that they sat down and rested. They were clearly tired and pleased to find a comfortable seat.

'I'm outside the cells now, sir,' Ahmed whispered down the phone. 'Cell two has a Conrad Sweetman in it.'

'Yes. That's the one. What's he up to?'

'I'll have to peer through the food-hatch in the door, sir,' Ahmed said tentatively.

'Well do it, lad,' Angel snapped. 'Do it now!'

There was silence.

'Well, what can you see? Is he still there?'

There was another short silence. Then Ahmed whispered: 'He's on the bunk asleep, sir.'

'Are you sure?'

'He's wearing a red dicky-bow.'

Angel sighed. 'Yes, that's him.'

'Yes, sir. He's snoring.'

Angel nodded. He wasn't pleased. He had half-hoped he wouldn't be there.

'Right, Ahmed. Thanks, lad.'

He closed the mobile and blew out a length of breath.

He turned to Gawber.

'Sweetman's fast asleep . . . in his cell.'

'Funny thought, sir,' Gawber said. 'You don't suppose there are two of them, do you? Conrad Sweetman and . . . his twin brother?'

Angel shook his head.

'No. One's bad enough! We'll find out very soon.' He looked at his watch. 'What time do you make it?'

Gawber pulled up his jacket sleeve.

'4.30, sir. Straight up.'

Angel nodded. He leaped across the room to the door to the hall. He saw a key in the door and locked it. There were some heavy maroon curtains at each side of the door, presumably there to reduce draughts. He closed them, stepped back and looked at his handiwork. Then he turned to the small gathering and said, 'We should take up positions as far away from that door and these windows as we can. I should sit down or better still lie on the floor. I don't think we'll have long to wait.'

★   ★   ★

He was right.

Three minutes later there was a loud bang that came from the hall.

The door shook. The windows rattled.

Mrs Hargreaves let out a cry.

Angel stood up. His pulse was racing. He looked at her and pointed to the house telephone.

'Dial 999. Send for the fire-brigade. Then

215

stay in here. And keep that door closed.'

'Yes, sir,' she said. She was shaking but she understood and reached out for the phone.

'Come on everybody,' Angel roared. He dashed over to the door, tore back the curtains, turned the key and pulled open the door.

He was first into the hall. The other five men were close behind. They ran into a blue mist, the smell of burning phosphorus, and a continuous hissing noise like a steam-engine waiting in the station. A cloud of smoke was emanating from a white incendiary bomb about sixteen inches long on the marble floor at the bottom of the staircase. It was spitting out sulphurous molten white heat from its tail, like a giant Roman candle, while throbbing and jumping irregularly like an eel out of water.

Around the rest of the room flames were flickering and flaring up dangerously on the carpet, curtains and wallpaper, making the sound of a strong wind and the snapping of dry twigs.

'Ron, come with me,' Angel yelled, shielding his eyes. 'The rest of you, do what you can. Ron, let's try and get this thing into the bath.'

He grabbed a shovel and Gawber took a spade. Between them they managed to roll the bomb on to the shovel and lift it into the galvanized bath of water. The bomb immediately bounced out like a snake. They repeated the action and at last managed to secure it in the bottom of the bath by holding it down with the shovel and spade. The bright, white flame still spewed out even under water.

The other men were smothering out flames on the carpet, walls and curtains with wet cushions and sacking and by stamping their feet on the carpet.

'You, lad,' Angel yelled to one of them near by. 'Pour that sack of sand on top of this bomb while we hold it down.'

The young constable nodded.

There was a splash as sand hit the water and made a muddy mixture.

'More,' Angel yelled.

The constable poured in another sackful, making a thicker mixture. At last the bomb stopped burning and surrendered in the mud. Gawber and Angel went to the aid of the others, using their shovel and spade to smother the flames.

The sulphur in the air was hard on the throat and eyes but everybody persevered and seemed to be winning the battle.

After a few minutes there was a hard banging on the front door.

Gawber went to open it.

It was the fire-brigade.

A man in a bright-yellow suit and brass helmet appeared. He rushed in, gaped round the blackened hall, rushed out, yelled something and came back with a dozen men armed with pick-axes and a heavy hose.

Angel took a deep breath and said: 'I think the fire's out, chaps. But we can leave you to dampen down and make it safe. Have you got a ladder?'

'A ladder, sir?'

'A very long ladder,' Angel said, wiping his eyes.

★ ★ ★

The following morning Angel drove into Bromersley police car-park and pulled up on a marked-out space next to the *Gaimster & Gibson, ventilation engineers* white Ford van and wondered why it always seemed to be in the space next to his. He made his way up the corridor and arrived promptly in his office at 8.28 a.m. He had hardly touched the post on his desk when the phone rang.

He reached out for the handset.

'Angel.'

It was superintendent Harker.

'Come on down, lad, a minute.'

'Right, sir.'

He replaced the phone and made his way to the monster's office.

'Good morning, sir. You wanted to see me?'

'Ah, there you are,' Harker said. He had his finger in his mouth trying to extricate a piece of bacon from between his teeth. 'Hmm. Come in, lad. Sit down. Sit down. Did you have a good night?'

Angel blinked. It was unusual for Angel to receive any sort of a cordial welcome from him. Asking about his welfare was rare indeed, and therefore he knew he must be wary.

'Yes, sir.'

'Good. Good,' said Harker heartily. Then significantly he added: 'So did the prisoner, Sweetman.'

Angel's eyebrows shot up.

It's a good job I didn't release Sweetman like you tried to persuade me to do. God knows where he might have disappeared to,' Harker said scornfully.

Angel felt as comfortable as an OAP listening to the Arctic Monkeys playing *The Old Rugged Cross.*

'He wouldn't have got far, sir,' he muttered with a sniff.

'Well, he certainly wouldn't have come anywhere where *you* were, would he? Thankfully, due to my foresight, he is safely locked up here.'

'Yes, and he isn't going to light up as much as a two-watt bulb on a keyring for the next ten or twelve years, I reckon,' Angel said grandly. Then feeling even more confident, he added: 'It has certainly exonerated Lee Wong.'

Harker ran his hand hard over his small bony chin. 'I never seriously thought that *that* young man could have included arson and murder in his list of minor crimes. Just wanted to keep you on your toes, lad. I expect you realized that.'

Angel could have spat in his eye.

'There is one serious question of discipline, however,' Harker said, 'arising out of the operation.'

Angel frowned. He couldn't imagine who could be in trouble. Yesterday's operation had gone as smoothly as Robin Cousins on an ice rink. He couldn't think of anybody who might have deserved disciplinary action.

'Oh yes, sir. Against whom?'

'Against you, lad, of course.'

Angel frowned.

'The chief fire-officer complained that you conned his men into erecting a ladder up to the very highest point in the ceiling and then, despite his protestations, you scrambled up it like a monkey . . . all the way to the top. And when he tried to stop you and instructed you to come down, you swore at him.'

Angel conceded that it was partly true.

'I didn't *swear* at him, sir.'

'He actually said you used a four letter word . . . followed by the word 'off'.'

'Well, I wanted to see the exact position where Sweetman had attached the bomb, sir. There were still traces of glue on the plasterwork. *Buzz* off is what I actually said, sir.'

Harker shook his head then rubbed a hand over his mouth. 'Be thankful there weren't any witnesses. I shall take your word for it, lad, of course. Think no more about it.'

Angel had not intended thinking any more about it.

'It was a devilish plan,' he said quickly. 'It was, of course, at the highest point in the ceiling of the house, strategically positioned to allow maximum drop down the stairwell. Sweetman had carefully selected MPs who lived in three-storey houses with similar architectural features. That's why the bombs always landed at the bottom of the main staircase.'

'Pity you didn't spot it when you searched the house,' Harker said drily.

'Well, it was placed very high up . . . at the very top of the ceiling and Sweetman had cunningly painted it white so that it would match the colour of the décor.'

Harker wrinkled his nose.

'And I suppose he put it up there when he came to each house posing as a gasman?'

'Yes, sir. At each house, on each occasion, exactly two days before he posted the letters.'

'Ah!' Harker gave a sniff. 'Sweetman threatened the MPs with arson if they *didn't* introduce legislation to rescind all the present drug laws, didn't he? Supposing Pennyfeather *had* proposed the introduction of such legislation? What would Sweetman have done in such a case?'

'But it never was a serious possibility, was it? Nobody in their right mind would vote for a drugs free-for-all when they knew the dreadful things drugs did to people, especially the young. Sweetman knew that none of the MPs he challenged could possibly agree to his demands. He was on a certainty.'

Harker nodded in agreement.

'What about the missing Chinaman, Lee Wong?'

'Still heard nothing, sir. His father thought he would return when he found out that he was no longer under suspicion.'

'Let's hope it works out like that for them. Hmmm. Well, that about wraps it up.'

Angel stood up to go.

'Better get all the stuff over to the CPS, ASAP.'

'There's just the little matter of the gas-company lorry, sir.'

'Oh yes. Any idea what Sweetman has done with it?'

'I think it is hidden in Mrs Buller-Price's copse, sir. And I am hopeful that it will have his dabs all over it.'

12

Angel stopped the BMW outside the farmhouse gate and was surprised to see that the front door was wide open. That was very unusual. It had not happened before. He pulled on the hand-brake and switched off the engine. The closing of the car door seemed to be the cue for Mrs Buller-Price's squad of five dogs to start barking. They came belting out of the house through the open door and surrounded him, yapping and wanting him to acknowledge them and give them a pat. He knew them well enough from past visits so they weren't a problem. But he was concerned for Mrs Buller-Price. He pushed through them quickly to the front gate and through the open door. The dogs yapped and barked and heralded him in excitedly.

'Mrs Buller-Price!' he called. 'Are you there? It's Inspector Angel. Are you all right? Mrs Buller-Price!'

'Ah!' she called out weakly. 'In the sitting-room, Inspector. Come through. Please come through!'

He found the old lady looking very pasty,

seated on the settee under a mountain of blankets and eider-downs. She was breathing heavily. The calling out had taken her breath, but she smiled broadly as he came into the room.

The room was never tidy, but today it was very much worse.

She pointed to the easy-chair opposite her and he sat down.

The dogs settled wherever they chose and flopped on the dusty carpet.

Angel looked at her closely.

'Looks to me as if you should be in hospital.'

'No. I can be in pain here more comfortably than in a hospital. But I am in need of the doctor. Dr Lemon is coming again this morning. Those new powerful painkillers she's prescribed make me drowsy. Can't do with that. I've my dogs and my Jerseys to see to.'

'Is the pain still in your back?'

'Yes. Yes. But I am sure it will go. One thing I have learned in life is that nothing (good or bad) lasts for ever. Mr Lestrange from the garage is milking the cows, in a fashion, and taking the churns to the gate for me. And seeing to their feeding . . . and the dogs. Those are the most important jobs.'

She straightened the sheet and blankets across her chest and then looked up at him and smiled. 'Now how are you, dear Inspector Angel? I should be making you some tea. I regret that I have no fresh baking to offer you.'

He smiled back.

'Wouldn't hear of it. You need professional attention.'

'No. If it doesn't subside soon, my niece in Chesterfield has said she will come up and look after me . . . there really is nothing for you to worry about, dear Inspector.'

Angel wondered whether to mention the matter of the missing items, her cat, the keys, the flour and the frying-pan.

'Have you discovered who your sneak thief is?' he said gently.

She sighed and looked down.

'Alas, no. A tin of plums has gone walkabout, Inspector.'

Angel frowned and shook his head.

'A tin of plums?'

'I fancied them with some packet custard for my tea. I asked Mr Lestrange if he would kindly reach the tin down from the top pantry shelf, but they were not to be found.'

Angel thought that that was indeed a mystery, and it thoroughly confounded him. The missing plums off the top shelf tended to discount the theory that the thief was a small child.

'So that's the keys, the flour, the frying-pan and now a tin of plums. And that's all that has gone missing?'

'No. No. The most valuable of all is my cat, Tulip.'

'Of course. You are sure that there isn't a way into the house that you are not aware of?'

'No. It's impossible. I've lived here over forty years. I know every brick and every tile.'

He rubbed his chin. He needed to move on.

'I am sure that I will solve the mystery in due course, Mrs Buller-Price,' he said. 'I shall put my mind to it, and if needs be, I will send up a constable to observe the house for twenty-four hours.'

She smiled briefly, then winced with pain. Her eyes closed.

'Thank you, Inspector. But it hasn't got as desperate as that, yet.'

'Now, if you are sure that I can do nothing to assist you . . . on the domestic front?'

She opened her eyes, waved a hand and quietly said: 'No thank you. Everything has been taken care of for the moment.'

'Now on another matter, I'm sorry to bother you, but my super is concerned . . . can you tell me if you still have that trespasser in your copse?'

She shook her head.

'I really don't know, Inspector.' She

yawned. 'Excuse me, Inspector. It's the pills. They make me tired and sleepy all the time. Since my back went, I have not been bothering to look out with my binoculars. But I tell you what, as you leave, not that I am pushing you off, you know, but when you leave, if you step up on to the platform where I leave my milk-churns for collection at the gate, you will be tall enough to see the copse and whether there is any vehicle up there.'

'Thank you, dear Mrs Buller-Price,' he said.

She didn't reply. She was fast asleep.

★ ★ ★

'Come in,' Angel called.

It was Crisp. He was carrying two fawn-coloured paper files.

Angel glared at him.

'There you are, lad,' he bawled. 'I've had Ahmed looking all over for you. Is there something the matter with your mobile?'

'I think it's on the blink, sir.'

Angel slid his eyes across to him suspiciously and said, 'You'd better get it fixed damned quick or else I'll have you on the blink.'

Crisp knew it was a warning. He licked his lower lip.

Angel pointed to the chair.

'Sit down. I want to get back to this Imelda Wilde case. Have SOCO finished?'

'Yes, sir. Got it here,' he said, waving the files. I've been through everything. The murder weapon was thought to be an ordinary serrated kitchen-knife. Didn't see anything much else there to help us.'

'I'll have a look at it later. Have you been through all her stuff?'

Crisp nodded and opened a file.

Angel remembered something.

'Did you come across an ugly-looking foreign doll, made from wood and material? She bought it at an auction last Saturday, for a damned silly price. I was there.'

'A doll? No, sir. Nothing like that.'

'Ugly thing. Did you see anything in her house to do with . . . fortune-telling . . . the occult . . . witchcraft?'

Crisp smiled.

'Oh. You mean crystal balls, tarot-cards, stuff like that?'

Angel nodded.

'No sir. And I would have noticed, because I'd heard the rumours that she was a witch, a white witch.'

Angel's eyebrows went up momentarily. He shook his head.

'Aye, well, we're not in the rumours

business, lad,' he said with a sniff. 'Did you find anything at all that might be useful?'

'A couple of things, sir. I got her Bromersley Building Society book. She's had as much as twenty odd thousand in there. But it's gone down and down. She made her last withdrawal on 1 March. Her balance there now is zero. And I found her bank-statement, and she's bumping on the bottom. Her last balance was one hundred and eighty pounds. Although it showed that she has made regular deposits of between a hundred and two hundred pounds a week. There was forty pounds in her purse. Yet she's not entitled to a state pension, there are no records of a private pension or any shares or bonds or any other sources of income, and she's not in anybody's employment.'

Angel frowned.

'She does some cleaning and helping at Fred Butcher's,' Angel said, 'but I don't suppose that would keep her in tights.'

'SOCO found two hundred pounds in cash in that registered packet addressed to her that you signed for.'

'Two hundred pounds? The postman who found her body said that she received registered packets frequently . . . they could all contain cash, I suppose.'

'If she got one every week, that would explain the regular bank-deposits.'

'And who is paid regularly besides the rent-man and the building society?' Angel said meaningfully.

Crisp frowned, then brightened as the penny dropped.

'A blackmailer, sir.'

Angel's jaw tightened.

'What did SOCO say about the packet?'

'They reported no clear fingerprints. No sender's name on the envelope. Apparently it's not mandatory. But they did find out that it came via a post office in Leeds.'

Angel screwed up his eyes and nodded slowly.

'Leeds, eh? Hmmm. Right, lad. Does she own the house?'

'No, sir. It's on a weekly rent from the Branksby estate. She pays it by standing order. Thank goodness, that's up to date.'

'Still, she'd be pretty hard up. Anything else?'

'Yes, sir,' he said grandly, and he opened the other fawn file and took out a folded piece of newspaper that had become a milk-chocolate-brown colour with age. 'I found this tucked in an envelope with her birth certificate and her parents' death certificates. I haven't had the opportunity to take it any further. Very interesting, I thought, sir.'

Angel grunted, took it from him and carefully unfolded it. The paper was thin and brittle; it was a page torn from a tabloid newspaper. In the top right-hand corner was printed; 'Northern Daily News Chronicle — 28 February 1981'.

A box had been roughly drawn by a red pen around a short news item in the middle of the page. The headline read:

DRIVER FINDS GIRL'S NAKED BODY

A crane-driver has discovered the naked body of a young female who appeared to have died from a knife wound to the chest.

The body was discovered as the workman was unloading a wagon of sand from a train in Crewe on Monday.

The police believe she met her death a few days ago, and subsequently was at some point put on the train which began its journey in Tyneside on Saturday, 23rd, crossed North Yorkshire and Lancashire and ended in Crewe in Cheshire on Sunday, 24th.

The young woman was dark-haired, aged between sixteen and twenty-four years.

The police are anxious to trace her identity. If you have any information, please telephone Crewe police on Crewe 1234 or contact any police officer.

Angel sniffed, then looked at the wall while rubbing the lobe of his ear between his finger and thumb. Then suddenly he reached out for the phone and dialled a number.

Ahmed answered.

'PC Ahaz here. Can I help you, sir?'

'Yes, Ahmed,' he said. 'Phone the main police station in Crewe. I want to speak to the duty-officer.'

'Yes, sir,' Ahmed said.

Angel replaced the phone and turned back to Crisp.

'Was there anything else, lad? Gold, cash, drugs, stolen goods, porn, guns, weapons. You know what rings my bell.'

'Nothing unusual or worth mentioning, sir.'

Angel sighed.

'Right, well, listen up. Butcher had all his girl assistants dressed to his requirements by a costumier known as Madame Rita of Harehills Road, Leeds. As far as I know, she's still there. Find her and get a list of every girl he ever sent to her to be measured for a costume or alterations. It'll go back a bit and

233

I expect there'll be quite a few, but be thorough and get every name. Right?'

'Right, sir,' Crisp said and made for the door.

'Now I want that first thing Monday morning.'

'Right, sir.'

Angel got up to leave.

'And keep in touch. Get a new mobile if that one's dicky, and let me have the number.'

'Yes, sir.'

Crisp grabbed the doorknob.

Angel suddenly had an idea.

'Hang on a minute, lad. Before you go, there's something else you could usefully do for me in Leeds. It's not exactly conventional police procedure. In fact it's a bit delicate, but you're the very man for it. You don't have to, of course. It's a bit beyond the regular call of duty. But I daresay you could enjoy it.'

Crisp turned back and stared at him. His boss never normally trespassed into personal or indelicate areas. This was very unusual. Crisp was intrigued. He wondered what secrets Angel could possibly have in Leeds? He rubbed his chin.

Angel grinned at him. 'Sit down, lad. There's fifty quid in it, for you, if you take it on. You could call it expenses,' he added ruefully.

Crisp smiled.

Fred Butcher showed Angel into the big room and closed the door. 'Back so soon, Inspector? You *must* be making progress,' he said with a bright smile. 'Please sit down.'

'Thank you, sir,' said Angel lowering himself into one of the two easy-chairs facing the window that had the long, uninterrupted view to the Pennines. 'Just a couple of questions, Mr Butcher. You have no doubt kept a record of all the theatres and places you played as the Great Mysto?'

Butcher smiled confidently.

'Yes, indeed I have. Why?'

'That would be from about 1970?'

'About then, yes. I didn't keep the unedifying date-books of the early days when I was scratching a living playing as Fred Butcher, the magic-man,' he said with a grin. 'Didn't have the same resonance as the Great Mysto, somehow.'

Angel nodded and smiled politely.

'No, I suppose not. I need to know where you were playing at a particular time.'

Butcher's eyebrows shot up.

'Really? Whatever for? I would need to look it up, of course.'

'It's for the period from the twenty-second of February to about the twenty-fourth, 1981.'

Butcher's face didn't even flicker.

'Give me a few minutes, and I'll let you know,' he said. 'Anything else, Inspector?'

'Yes. I'd like you to give me a list of all the young women in your employ from 1970 to the date you retired.'

'Phew. That's a tall order.'

'With your attention to detail I'm sure it won't be difficult.'

Butcher didn't look happy. He rubbed his chin and screwed up his eyes. 'You're going back a long time. What's it all about?'

'Just routine,' Angel lied.

Butcher didn't believe him.

Angel knew it, but it suited his purpose. He eyed the old man carefully, and to take him off guard deliberately, added, 'By the way, do you know if Imelda Wilde was blackmailing anybody?'

That was a question Butcher hadn't expected.

His mouth opened slightly, then closed. His eyes moved uncertainly.

'I'm sure she isn't . . . wasn't, blackmailing anybody,' he stammered.

★ ★ ★

'The Eastern Power and Gas Company construction vehicle, sir?' Angel said.

236

'Yes, lad,' Harker growled. 'I thought you said that Buller-Price woman knew something about it?'

'An attempt was made to hide it in the trees, on Mrs Buller-Price's land, without permission, sir, that's all. I was up there this morning. It was there then. Mrs Buller-Price is not at all well; she's not been able to monitor all its comings and goings. I have asked SOCO to check it out and recover it. It must be the vehicle Sweetman stole. I am hopeful they can connect him to it. That'll sew that case up nice and sweetly. I've got DS Gawber liaising with SOCO and following it through.'

Harker sniffed, then lifting his head up, and said: 'Yes. I'd like to be able to phone the chairman . . . tell him I've found his firm's vehicle, and return it to him. Hmm. I'll have a word with SOCO myself later. Right. Now how are you getting along with this Wilde murder?'

'It's moving, sir. It's moving. I've spoken to Crewe police about that old newspaper report. They say that although the body of the young woman was never identified, they were able to tell me that she was four months pregnant and that, from her general physical condition, particularly her leg muscles, they thought at the time that she was a full-time professional athlete or a dancer. Also that the wound in her chest appeared to have been made by an ordinary serrated kitchen-knife.'

Harker frowned.

'When was this?'

'February 1981.'

'February 1981?' bawled Harker, pulling one of his best Boris Karloff faces. 'What the hell are we doing wasting time on a case in Crewe that happened more than a quarter of a century ago? We've enough cases of our own; there's no need for you to go out touting for more . . . like a brush-salesman?'

Angel's lips tightened.

'There might be similarities with the Wilde case, sir,' he said patiently.

'*Might be?*' Harker roared. 'Only *might* be? Drop that line of enquiry, lad. We've enough on here solving our own cases. I can't see what good it would do us helping Crewe with their clear-up rate. They've never done anything for us.'

Angel nodded but he had absolutely no intention of doing anything of the kind. The lead was far too promising to drop. And if he proved to be right, he knew that Harker would conveniently forget all about this directive.

Angel had to field a few more questions from the incredible hulk before he was able to

238

escape. Then he beat a hasty retreat up the corridor to his own office and closed the door. He slumped in the chair, leaned back in it and stared at the ceiling. He was certain that if he could discover who had murdered the unknown girl and dumped her on the goods train, back in February 1981, he would also know the identity of the murderer of Imelda Wilde. His plan to achieve that was already in progress. By Monday morning it should have moved on to the interesting stage. He was still staring at the ceiling, considering his next move when the church clock rang out the Westminster chime and struck five.

It was the end of another imperfect week. He was glad to be going home.

★   ★   ★

It was 8.28 a.m., Monday 17 April and Angel positively bounced down the green corridor. He was still boldly carrying the umbrella (and rice) that he had taken from Sweetman's only six days previously. (It seemed like a year ago, so much had happened during those last few days). He was eager to get back to work, and bursting with the certainty that he was going to arrest the murderer of Imelda Wilde in the next couple of days.

He stashed the brolly between the pipe and the wall and then swivelled round to face his desk. The post had already arrived and was in a small pile in front of him. This morning there had been an unusually thin delivery. The only letter marked personally to him had a Leeds postmark and was franked with Max Starr's name. He tore open the envelope. Inside was a With Compliments slip fastened with a paperclip to an A4 sheet of paper with a list of girl's names printed out. He glanced down it. The names themselves meant nothing to him except for about three-quarters of the way down where he noticed the name of Imelda Wilde. He read down to the bottom and then counted the number of entries. There were twenty-four. He nodded with satisfaction and lowered the paper on to the desk.

There was a knock at the door.

'Come in.'

It was Crisp with a sheet of paper held out in front of him.

'Morning, sir. I've got that list from Madame Rita. I extracted the names from her invoice books. I have been through thousands of invoices, all in sequence, in date order, and I've included the date of the invoice. Of course, there were lots of later entries for Imelda Wilde.' He handed the paper to Angel.

'Ta, lad,' said Angel eagerly. He raced down it enthusiastically. It appeared to be pretty much identical in content to Max Starr's. Then he counted the number of girls' names and there were twenty-five. He nodded with great satisfaction. There was a difference. A very telling difference.

Angel looked up at Crisp.

'I think that here we have the name of the girl murdered in 1981.'

Together they checked off the two lists and the entry of a girl's name on Madame Rita's list which was not on Max Starr's list was a Fiona Frinton.

Angel's eyes flashed.

'Fiona Frinton. That'll be her! Look, lad,' Angel said urgently. 'See if you can find her on any missing persons list, dated shortly after the twenty-third of February 1981. She would then have been between sixteen and twenty-four years of age, brunette, four months pregnant and thought to be a professional athlete or a dancer.'

Crisp nodded and made for the door.

'And keep in touch,' he called.

'Right, sir.'

The door closed.

Angel leaned back in the chair and rubbed his chin slowly.

13

Angel carefully positioned the tip of the umbrella on the doorbell button and pushed. Seconds later Fred Butcher came to the door. He was smiling as he opened it, but the smile left him when he saw that it was Angel standing there.

'Good morning, Mr Butcher. Perhaps you could spare me a few minutes?' Angel said as sensitively as if he was addressing a new vicar.

'More questions. More questions,' Butcher grumbled. He hesitated, then pulled back the door and abruptly waved his visitor in. The old-world charm had gone.

'Will this never end?' Butcher continued.

'Oh yes, indeed, it will,' Angel replied confidently, smoothly slotting his brolly into the hallstand. 'Today, all being well, Mr Butcher. Today.'

Butcher frowned, which made him look like the wicked monster in a children's story-book.

They went through into the big room and Butcher pointed to a chair.

Angel sat down.

Butcher then ambled over to the big desk

in the corner and returned with a long book and a sheet of paper.

'I have spent almost the entire weekend getting out these names for you,' he said gruffly. 'I hope you will find them satisfactory.'

Angel took the sheet of paper from him. It was a list, neatly handwritten. He glanced down it swiftly, looking for a Fiona Frinton, which, as he expected, was not there. He counted the number of names on the list and it came to twenty-four.

He looked up at Butcher knowingly; he nodded and said, 'Thank you.'

Then Butcher waved the long book he was holding and said, 'This is my datebook for 1981. You wanted to know where I was playing week beginning Monday, the eighteenth of February to Saturday, the twenty-third of February.'

Angel nodded.

'We played to packed houses in the Theatre Royal, Blackchester, North Yorkshire. I remember, there wasn't an empty seat in the house.'

'Thank you,' Angel said politely.

He turned over a page.

'And the week after that, we were in York. That also . . .'

Angel put up a hand.

'That's all I need, Mr Butcher, thank you.'

Butcher pulled a face, closed the book noisily, trundled over to the far end of the room, placed it on the desk, then came to the chair next and at ninety degrees to Angel and settled down into it.

'You've some more questions for me?' he said grumpily.

Angel started gently. When aiming for a confession he always tried to create an easy, friendly, reasonable approach, if possible.

'I hope you can help me, Mr Butcher. You will understand that we get all sorts of people to deal with down at the police station. We get a lot of crooks, of course, and we have recently arrested a man for stealing a book and trying to sell it in a public house, the Feathers, actually. It was a very old book, leather-bound, called a grimoire, dated 1646. I know nothing about these things. We always have to put a monetary value on everything stolen. Now one of my officers told me that you would know about this particular subject.'

Butcher was smiling; either Angel had successfully managed to massage his ego or he was intensely interested in the subject matter; or both.

'I am no authority, Inspector. I know a little. What . . . what is the title of the book, exactly?'

'It is called *Dowdeswell's Book of Magick Spells*.'

Butcher's eyes lit up: the smile widened.

'Sounds fascinating. I really must see it.'

Angel also smiled. He thought he might get in close proximity to it much more quickly than ever he could have imagined.

'I should think it is quite valuable . . . but it would depend on its condition, whether it is the genuine article and so on,' added Butcher.

'You are interested in witchcraft, the occult?'

'Very much so. You know, years ago magic and the occult were inseparable. The people believed that magicians were gifted with spiritual powers. That is still the case in parts of Africa and South America. In the civilized and educated world, however, everybody accepts that stage or television magicians are illusionists. I mean, we really don't saw women in half, do we? We simply appear to do the impossible and the illusion, presented well, makes for entertainment. Or it did. Also, no serious-minded person now believes in witches and warlocks. Although the people who make and sell all the modern, party stuff wouldn't necessarily agree. But I take an academic interest in it. It is an interest I can pursue here in my retirement. I find it very interesting. I have let it be known that I am in the market for old, genuine occult paraphernalia. If I can buy enough, maybe I will open a museum somewhere. I don't believe there is one, anywhere in the world. No harm in that, is there?'

'No. None,' Angel had to agree. 'Was Imelda Wilde interested in witchcraft.'

'No. I'm sure not. Why?'

'She bought an ugly doll, a shapeless, nondescript lump of wood and rags with a brightly painted face, at an auction a week last Saturday for some ridiculous price. After her death her house was searched. It wasn't there. It was nowhere to be found.'

Butcher smiled gently.

'She bought it on my account. She knew I would be interested in it. It's a poppet. The sort of thing you stick pins in to get your own back on an opponent or enemy. She gave it to me. I reimbursed her, of course. I have it in my study.'

Angel nodded. That cleared that up. He was satisfied with the explanation.

Butcher looked down at the floor. Angel noticed and thought that he seemed sad. He rubbed his chin before continuing.

'There is something much more serious I would like to draw to your attention.'

Butcher looked up.

'I want to take you back to a Saturday night in February 1981. To the Theatre Royal, Blackchester.'

Butcher's eyes jumped and then settled under half-closed lids.

'Did you and Imelda share the bill that night with anyone else?'

'I shouldn't think so. No, I'm certain of it. By then we were doing the entire two hours and ten minutes by ourselves. We had enough material to do up to three hours if necessary . . .'

'Just the two of you?'

'Yes.'

'And in your programme, do you happen to remember if you included the Caliph and the Slave Girl illusion?'

He smiled.

'Yes. Almost certainly. Fancy you remembering things like that. You must have paid close attention to the act. We used to end the show with it. It became our speciality. The audience used to send us off to rapturous applause.'

Angel nodded.

'I've seen you do it live on television. That's where you played the part of the Caliph and Imelda took the part of the slave girl.'

'Yes,' Butcher said smiling.

'It's where you brought on two trestles and

a fancy jewelled coffin-shaped box, which was clearly empty. You chased Imelda round the stage in an attempt to blindfold her. At first, you failed. She tried to hide behind a narrow pillar, but you could still see her, you found her, put on the blindfold, dragged her out, picked her up and put her screaming and kicking into the empty box and you eventually closed the lid.'

'Yes. Yes,' Butcher said, smiling. He was pleasantly surprised at Angel's accurate account of what happened, and was really enjoying the nostalgia.

'Then you wrapped a chain round the box several times, locked it and covered the box with a cloth?'

'Yes.'

'Seconds later, Imelda appeared from among the audience in the glare of a spotlight and a chord from the orchestra?'

'That's right. That's right,' said Butcher excitedly. 'Then I acted surprised, nay, amazed. Dashed over to the jewelled box, pulled off the cloth, unravelled the chain, opened the box and showed that it was empty. I then appeared to be even more amazed! And hey presto! The illusion was completed.' He clapped his hands several times and smiled, remembering the occasion. 'Happy days, Inspector. Happy days.'

Angel sighed, thought for a few seconds, rubbed his chin again and said, 'Not *so* happy, Mr Butcher. Not *so* happy.'

Butcher frowned. The smile was gone.

'That particular night . . . wasn't quite like that, was it?' Angel said slowly.

Butcher didn't reply.

'You have consistently told me that you never employed more than one girl at a time.'

Butcher still didn't reply.

'And there's no way that that illusion can be worked without using a second girl or a robot that has pretty legs and can kick them in the air. Well, even you haven't got a robot *that* good yet, have you?'

Butcher sat there attentively, watching, listening and thinking.

'This is what I think happened, Mr Butcher. Everything was exactly as I have said, excepting that there was another young woman, dressed and looking as much like Imelda as possible, hidden behind the pillar. She partly showed herself to the audience, an ankle, a bit of leg or an arm precisely at the moment Imelda arrived there and gave her the cue, so that the audience immediately believe that what they could see belonged to Imelda. Why shouldn't they? Then Imelda promptly climbed straight up the ladder fastened to the back of the scenery pillar to the gallery over the stage where the stagehands threw petals down on the fairy coach, and grunge on the comedian. She scrambled across that to the ladder in the wings, where she descended. She then went out through the stage door into the street, regardless of the weather, and back in through the front of the theatre and into the audience to await her cue from you, which, I believe, was when you turned away from fussily covering the trick box on the stage. Meanwhile, the second girl, shall we call her Fiona . . . '

Butcher's face told Angel all he wanted to know. His jaw dropped open. His mouth tried to form words.

'I thought you'd remember her, even though you didn't put her name on your list,' Angel bawled.

'No. No. It's not what you think,' said Butcher stammering.

Angel continued.

'Meanwhile Fiona Frinton had had her face covered with the blindfold and any disparity in her height, or any other difference, would have been unnoticed by the fact that you carried her to the trick box on the stage. After Imelda appeared to the audience in the theatre, and you showed the trick box to be empty, all Fiona had to do was lie doggo in the box's concealed compartment until you and Imelda had finished taking your bows and the proscenium curtains had finally closed.'

Angel stopped, stared at the man and said, 'You're a fraud, Mr Butcher, a liar and a murderer. After that particular Saturday night's performance, you stabbed Fiona Frinton, took her in your car to a bridge, twenty miles from the theatre, stripped her and threw her over a bridge on to a passing goods train. The train, on which she was eventually found in Crewe, had passed under that bridge that night. You've always insisted that you only had *one* girl at a time in the act when I knew it was impossible. You've told me one lie after another.'

Butcher looked across at him and said, 'That's not true, sir. What possible motive could I have had for killing that young woman?'

'You killed her because she had just told you that she was pregnant and that you were the father and you didn't want the responsibility and the awful publicity.'

Butcher smiled, but there was no joy in it.

'That's ridiculous. At that time, I was about forty-five, a confirmed bachelor, and she was twenty.'

'You *knew* she was pregnant?'

251

'Yes. Not at the time she was murdered, though, but later.'

'How did you find out?'

'I was told.'

'Who by.'

'Can't say.'

'You're lying again,' Angel bawled.

Butcher showed his teeth. He was angry.

'Have you never tried to respect someone's memory?'

'What are you talking about?' Angel growled.

'You wouldn't understand.'

'Try me. Or you'll go down for twenty years.'

'I was a respectable man . . . a well-known figure in the profession. In some quarters I was called 'Mr Magic'. I couldn't be seen to be associated with a twenty-year-old pregnant showgirl. A girl young enough to be my daughter. How would it have looked in the Sunday papers?'

'So you thought you would murder her to get rid of the evidence?'

'I didn't murder anybody. It was terrible, terrible!' Butcher said. He suddenly stood up.

Angel said: 'What are you doing? Sit down.'

'I want a drink,' Butcher said.

Angel nodded.

'So do I.'

'What do you want? Coffee?'

Angel nodded.

Butcher went out into the hall and along to the kitchen. Angel followed him. The making and serving of the coffee was a joint effort executed in silence. Butcher did most of the work; of course he knew where things were, and it was Butcher who carried the tray with the cups and coffee-pot back to the big room. He did the pouring and the passing, and when they had supped and refilled, he licked his lips, put his cup down on the saucer and turned to Angel.

'What you have said about the way the illusion worked was essentially correct, Inspector. I always tried to conceal the fact that there was a second girl involved, but that was to make the best of the illusion. I employed her and saved her for that one trick only. She didn't appear anywhere else in the show. She didn't get a credit in the programme or on the bill. I hope you will understand that that was professional deception and nothing more.'

He pushed the empty cup and saucer away. 'This is what actually happened. As usual, that night, everything had gone well. The audience had loved us, especially that last illusion. The curtain came down. Fiona had left the stage and gone when I reached the box and trestles. I moved them to a place near the door for collection the next day, and then went round the back to my dressing-room, which was one of three rooms along the end wall of the theatre furthest from the stage-manager's desk. The door to my room was closed. I opened it and found Fiona on the floor on her back, her chest covered in blood. It was ghastly. I quickly reached down and tried to find a pulse on her wrist and her neck. She was very warm, but there wasn't a pulse . . . *there wasn't one.* I realized that I must phone for an ambulance and the police. I dashed out to tell somebody. I was looking for the stage-manager. He had a phone. I passed Imelda's room next door. She saw me, I told her. She came back with me. She also tried to find a pulse on Fiona and couldn't. It was too late. We went back into Imelda's dressing-room. She had a bottle of something in her drawer. She let me have the plastic beaker. I had a good swig. She drank out of the bottle. We talked over what to do. She said that nothing could be achieved by calling in the police, and that my name and hers would be in all the papers . . . she also told me that Fiona was pregnant, it wouldn't look good . . . people would jump to conclusions. Fiona had always been a bit flighty. Also, there was blood on the dressing-room floor *and* on my

Caliph's costume, which would all have to be explained. There was no proof I hadn't stabbed her, so I was afraid and I agreed. We cleared Fiona's clothes and things from her dressing-room, undressed her, wrapped her in a spare cape of mine and moved her body into the wardrobe in the dressing-room. Imelda took her clothes and things and disposed of them. Then got changed. As it was Sunday the following day and the removal van would be coming to move our scenery and props on to York, I told the stage-manager I wanted to be in the theatre early, so it was not difficult to persuade him to let me borrow a key. We then went to the hotel where Imelda cleared the girl's room. In the middle of the night I came back to the theatre, collected her body and, as you have discovered, disposed of it over a railway bridge.'

14

Angel pulled his car on to a parking space on Fenton Street, just off The Headrow in Leeds. He fed the meter and strode briskly out on the busy pavement into the sunshine, using the umbrella as a walking-stick. He noticed the white Ford '*Gaimster & Gibson, ventilation engineers*' van parked near the entrance to Bramah Buildings and walked passed it without even giving it a glance. He went up the steps into the building, into the lift to the second floor. He turned right out of the lift and walked purposely down the corridor to Max Starr's office. He reached the glass door and walked in. The young woman with the big bosom was not there to greet him, so he walked straight past the unattended desk to the other glass door and opened it.

A surprised Max Starr looked up from his desk.

His appearance was exactly the same as before: coatless, shirt-sleeves rolled back, tobacco smoke singeing his eyebrows. When he saw it was Angel he stood up, dragged off his spectacles and pulled the cigar out of his mouth.

'Your receptionist . . . ' Angel was about to explain.

'Come in. Come in. Sit down,' Max Starr said with a smile. He nodded in the direction of the receptionist's room. 'I know. I know. Gone back to her mother's, I shouldn't wonder. Eh?' Then he forced a laugh.

If there was a joke there, Angel didn't appreciate it. He closed the door and sat down putting the umbrella across his lap.

Starr clenched his hands on his desk, leaned forward and said, 'You got my list?'

'Yes, thank you,' Angel said. 'I got your list. Unfortunately it was incomplete so it wasn't much use to me,' he said slyly.

Starr's mouth dropped open. The pupils of his eyes bounced.

'What do you mean?'

Angel pursed his lips then said: 'You forgot to include one of your old girl-friends.'

Starr's mouth dropped open. He shook his head.

'You've lost me.'

Angel sighed, then said: 'Don't let's play games, Mr Starr. I'm talking about Fiona Frinton.'

'Fiona Frinton? Fiona Frinton? Never heard of her. Look Inspector, I get hundreds, no thousands, of girls through here in the course of a month. We've got over two thousand on our books. This business has been in existence for almost seventy years. I've been here nearly thirty of them. I can't be expected to remember every girl who sails in here mad keen to be in showbusiness. If there was a Fiona Frinton assisting Fred Butcher, he would know about her. He recorded everything. Anyway, what's she got to do with anything? I thought you were investigating the murder of Imelda Wilde?'

'There are several similarities in the way the murders were committed. Whoever murdered Fiona Frinton also murdered Imelda Wilde.'

'So she was also murdered was she?'

'Yes.'

'Similarities? What sort of similarities?'

'Oh, different things,' Angel said quietly, and then he added, 'Imelda wasn't pregnant, if that's what you were wondering.'

The pupils of Starr's eyes bounced again. The left corner of his mouth twitched.

'But there are matters of DNA, of course. We only have to check the DNA of the foetus from the remains of the womb of Fiona Frinton and match it up to the DNA of the male partner, and there we have the murderer of Imelda Wilde. QED. Just like that.'

Starr's mind must have been in turmoil but he maintained a fixed expression.

'You are far too smart for me this morning, Inspector. Are you accusing me of something? If so, what?'

Angel nodded coolly.

'Yes, Mr Starr. That's exactly what I'm doing. I'm accusing you of the murders of Fiona Frinton *and* Imelda Wilde.'

Starr sniggered, puffed hard on the stub of the little cigar and said, 'You'll never prove it.'

Angel nodded.

'Oh yes. I believe we already have.'

'What evidence have you got? Don't give me that guff about DNA. It wouldn't still be around after twenty-five years.'

'How did you know the murder occurred twenty-five years ago if you've never heard of her?'

Starr didn't like that. He thought a moment. He'd made a big mistake.

'It was just a figure I plucked out of the air. A quarter of a century. It didn't mean anything specific. Anyway, to make a comparison, you'd need *my* DNA,' he said, his eyes shining. 'And I would withhold it.'

Angel shook his head slowly. He couldn't resist smiling.

'We've already got it,' he said quietly.

Starr's face changed. His eyes narrowed.

'You couldn't have.'

'One of your used cigar butts was all we

needed. Your friendly receptionist gave my officer the choice of those you smoked on Friday.'

Starr's eyes almost shot out of his head.

'Maureen!' he bawled.

'Yes. Maureen Clutterbuck, is her name I believe.'

'How do you know her name?'

'I asked her,' said Angel nonchalantly. 'She didn't mind telling me.'

'Where is she now?'

'Oh, she's safely out of your way. She's — I suppose you'd say — helping the police with their enquiries.'

Starr was shell-shocked. He stubbed out the cigar that was smouldering between his fingers.

Angel continued: 'Yes. She's explained how every Friday she took a registered packet that she saw you stuff with ten twenty-pound notes addressed to Imelda Wilde to post at the head post office. She'd done that every Friday since she came here two years ago. Until you unexpectedly stopped her, last Friday. I wonder why?'

'Imelda didn't need the money any more.'

'No, Max. That really won't do. Maureen listened in to the telephone call she made to you on Monday last, and it was clear that Imelda was blackmailing you and that that phone call was pressing you for an additional one hundred pounds a week.'

'And what hold could Imelda Wilde possibly have over me to make me pay her any money?'

'Come on, Max. Let's stop playing games. Know when you're licked. What you need is a good lawyer.'

Starr suddenly leaped up from the chair. He waved his arms in the air wildly.

'They are bitches,' he yelled. 'The whole lot of them. This Maureen is the latest of a long line of bitches. I promised her a holiday in Florida, for God's sake!'

'It started with Fiona, didn't it?'

Starr didn't reply at first. He walked over to the window and looked out of it without seeing anything. If he had got close enough to the glass he might have been able to see the roof of the white Ford '*Gaimster & Gibson, ventilation engineers*' van on the street below, where his every word was being listened to and recorded.

'She was the first, in fact, the only one I got up the duff. My father wouldn't stand for it. I would have had the kid and played happy families but my father talked me out of it. Fiona wouldn't make it easy. She wanted the kid. She wanted me to leave my father and the business, and start a life with her. But the

261

agency was all I knew. I was making a good screw. My dad would leave it to me eventually. Time was passing. Fiona was beginning to show. I was in the middle of a tug of war. Something had to give. I knew she was on tour with Mysto, the magic man. That was far enough away from here. I thought it would never be traced back here to me. Fred Butcher was having it cushy. He'd be blamed for it . . . '

'Where did you get the knife from?'

'The kitchen drawer at home.'

'You took it with you?'

Starr nodded.

'The same with Imelda?'

He nodded again.

'Of course, you'll never prove *any* of this. I was very careful. I wore gloves. Wiped the knives clean. No fingerprints. No footprints. Burned my gloves, suit, shirt and shoes. You've a bit of circumstantial evidence from Maureen, but you'd need an admission from my very own lips to make a case against me stick.'

Angel turned away, pulled his jacket away from his shirt by the lapel, looked down at where his left nipple would be and in a quiet voice said, 'I have got all we need, Ron. Come in, charge him and take him away.'

The door to the reception room opened

and Gawber and two uniformed constables came in.

★ ★ ★

In the afternoon of that same day Angel, on his way back from Leeds, turned off the MI and went up on the old Manchester Road to Tunistone. He stopped the BMW outside the farmhouse door and was pleased to note that on that day the front door was duly closed. He glanced around. The farmyard was deserted, and, apart from the occasional whine from a gusty spring breeze, it was unusually quiet. The wind on the Pennines could play eerie tricks on the ears.

He pulled on the hand-brake, closed the window and switched off the ignition. He had been concerned about the welfare of Mrs Buller-Price. When he had called there three days ago she had not looked at all well. He had been up to his eyes with work at the time, but now the pressure had eased, he intended to try to unmask Mrs Buller-Price's mysterious intruder and petty pilferer.

He reached out for a small brown-paper bag from the front seat and, picking up Sweetman's umbrella from the back, he got out of the car.

He took a step towards the house.

Then all hell broke loose. Mrs Buller-Price's five dogs appeared from round the corner of the barn, spotted him and started barking as they began the charge towards him.

Angel was not pleased at the impending assault, but he was cheered because he knew that Mrs Buller-Price would not be far away. Indeed, from around the corner, like an upmarket bag-lady, she appeared. She was walking slowly, panting and pushing on her long Derbyshire hiker's stick. She beamed when she recognized Angel and gave him a cheery wave.

Meanwhile, the dogs clustered around him and began the process of sniffing and exploring his knees, his shoes and the umbrella. Schwarzenegger, the largest of them all, a brindle Alsatian, shoved his wet nose into his hand to invite a friendly stroke.

When she reached her front gate Mrs Buller-Price said: 'Very nice to see you again, Inspector. You're just in time for tea.'

Angel nodded his thanks.

'And my dear old tom cat, Tulip is back. He's in charge again in the barn. Thank you for your trouble.'

'I'm very glad to hear it. I haven't done anything really.'

'Please thank the RSPCA for their effort.'

'I will. I can see that you are a lot better today, Mrs Buller-Price,' he said with a smile. 'You must let me into the secret.'

'I will,' she said mischievously as she opened the front door. The dogs squeezed their way roughly around her legs into the house.

She turned left into the kitchen and said, 'You go into the sitting-room, Inspector. You sit where Tony Curtis likes to sit. I'll put the kettle on.'

He smiled and knew where she meant. The room was much tidier than it had been the last time he was there, which confirmed that she was on better form. He chose the armchair facing the fireplace. He put the paper bag on the table and placed the umbrella across his lap.

The dogs flopped anywhere they liked and fell instantly asleep, or pretended to.

It was not very long before Mrs Buller-Price arrived with the tray.

'Thank you, Mrs Buller-Price. I can see you are back to your usual good health. How did you manage it?'

Before she sat down, she reached up to the mantelshelf, took down a small bottle and handed it to him.

'I owe it all to these pills,' she said meaningfully.

Angel raised his eyebrows and tried to read the label. It was a long name and impossible to read out aloud.

'Taking these pills cured your back?' he enquired brightly.

'*No*,' she said loudly and frowned. '*Stopping* taking those pills cured my back! I am as fit as a fiddle now.'

He thought he understood what was meant; he was considering whether to seek clarification or let it go. He sipped the tea and decided on the latter.

'The doctor came to see me, shortly after you left, last Friday. She examined me, went through all my symptoms and then told me not to take any more of those pills. Apparently one of the side-effects of them is loss of memory. That's what was happening to me. I was doing things and forgetting all about them.'

Angel nodded. Realization dawned.

'You found the plums, the keys, the flour . . . '

'I found *everything*. I had apparently been doing things and moving things around and forgetting all about it. I am so grateful to you for listening to me and understanding.'

'I am only pleased at the happy outcome.'

'Now you must have a piece of my Battenburg.'

'I have brought you some grapes,' said Angel, handing her the paper bag.

'Oh. How very nice,' she said with her usual delightful smile.

★   ★   ★

There was a knock at the door.

'Come in.'

It was Gawber.

'Yes, Ron?'

'Just had a phone message for you, sir. But your line was engaged. It was from Mr Wong. Harry Wong.'

'Oh yes? What did he want?'

'He wanted to tell you that his son, Lee, saw the report of the arrest of Sweetman on the arson charge in last Saturday morning's papers, and came straight back home. He had been working in the kitchen of a London hotel. Mr and Mrs Wong and his wife are delighted with the outcome and want to thank you for your understanding.'

Angel nodded. He felt a little sorry for them. Then he smiled.

'Also,' Gawber said, 'I am sure you'd like to know, sir, that SOCO have been all over the Eastern Power and Gas Company vehicle, and that it has Sweetman's prints on the wheel and a door handle.'

Angel nodded.

'That's great, Ron. Sews that up a treat. That evidence will assure the CPS's barrister of an easy ride. There's more than enough to get a guilty verdict of arson *and* manslaughter.'

Gawber turned to go.

Angel said: 'And when SOCO can release the vehicle, inform the super. He wants the glory of arranging for its return to the gas company.'

Gawber grinned.

'Then finish off the Sweetman case report for the CPS and let me have a look at it,' Angel said.

The grin left Gawber's face.

'Today, sir?' he queried in shocked surprise.

'Why not?'

Gawber wrinkled his nose.

'I'll do what I can,' he said and made for the door.

He reached the door, then turned back. 'Don't forget that brolly, sir,' he said, pointing at the umbrella standing wedged behind the silver-painted radiator pipe, behind Angel's chair.

Angel frowned, then understanding him, he nodded.

'Aye. Thanks, Ron. Tell Ahmed I want him.'

'Right, sir.'

The door closed.

Angel rubbed his chin and his eyes caught the pile of post in front of him. He really would have to get down to it. He began to riffle through it.

There was a knock at the door.

'Come in.'

It was Ahmed.

'You wanted me, sir?'

'Yes, lad,' he said, and he swivelled round on the chair to the radiator pipe behind him, pulled out the umbrella that he had taken from Sweetman's house only six long days ago. He handed it to Ahmed and said, 'Here lad. Put a label on that, mark it 'Exhibit CS6' and take it round to the CPS office straightaway. And you'd better point out to them that there's rice inside it. Hold it upright. Don't go spilling the stuff on *my* carpet.'

Ahmed took the umbrella and felt the handle. He gripped it tightly. Clearly he enjoyed the feel of it.

Angel noticed.

'Go on, lad. Crack on with it. We've a lot to do.'

Ahmed hesitated, frowned, looked at Angel and said, 'You know, sir, I've read all the reports and statements to do with this arson and manslaughter case, but I still don't understand. The umbrellas . . . Whatever was the point of the umbrellas with rice in them, being stuck up on the ceiling in Sweetman's bedroom?'

Angel leaned back in his chair. He shook his head and ran his tongue along his bottom lip.

'You weren't following carefully enough, were you?'

Ahmed smiled at him. He knew he was being teased.

'That umbrella was weighed on scales in Harry Wong's kitchen. Including the rice, it weighed six pounds, ten and a half ounces, which I remembered was exactly the weight of the BZ2 Incendiary Bomb.'

Ahmed stood there rubbing his chin.

'It was simply a timing-device, lad. He put rice in the brolly to make each one weigh the same as the bomb, and then stuck them up on the ceiling to see how long they would take to fall.'

Ahmed's jaw dropped. Then his eyes lit up. He looked at Angel and smiled.

'That's fantastic, sir. I don't know how you do it, sir. It's fantastic!'

We do hope that you have enjoyed reading this large print book.

Did you know that all of our titles are available for purchase?

We publish a wide range of high quality large print books including:
Romances, Mysteries, Classics
General Fiction
Non Fiction and Westerns

Special interest titles available in large print are:
The Little Oxford Dictionary
Music Book
Song Book
Hymn Book
Service Book

Also available from us courtesy of Oxford University Press:
Young Readers' Dictionary
(large print edition)
Young Readers' Thesaurus
(large print edition)

For further information or a free brochure, please contact us at:
Ulverscroft Large Print Books Ltd.,
The Green, Bradgate Road, Anstey,
Leicester, LE7 7FU, England.
Tel: (00 44) **0116 236 4325**
Fax: (00 44) **0116 234 0205**

Other titles published by
The House of Ulverscroft:

MANTRAP

Roger Silverwood

Detective Inspector Michael Angel is on the trail of a serial murderer in the South Yorkshire town of Bromersley. The only common factor linking the victims is their association with the late Lord Ogmore. There are no clues, no fingerprints, no DNA — and Angel's only witness is blind . . . A glamorous schoolmistress with a past, two men with ponytails, a set of needle-sharp silver-handled stilettos and a fluffy toy elephant all play their part in the scramble to find the killer.